WHERE'S NINA?

SAUL WARSHAW

Full Moon Publishing, LLC
Glade Spring, VA
fullmoonpublishingllc.com
Cover image by Lee Helton

ISBN: 978-1-946232-28-1

Other Works by Saul Warshaw

CONTENTS

ACKNOWLEDGMENTS

If you are a major league baseball fan, you have probably heard about Shohei Ohtani, the Los Angeles Angels multi-talented pitcher and hitter – the first player to handle both roles in some 50 years.

Well, I've been blessed with a similar, multi-talented person. His name is Rob Stock. And he has been of incredible help in my writing of *Where's Nina*, as well as the other Will Jonas Mystery books, and two other novels, *Instinct for Survival and Where's Nina.*

First reader, grammarian, proofreader, story line suggester, general encourager, good friend – these are the talents that Rob applies, for my benefit.
Thank you, Rob!

Saul Warshaw

CHAPTER ONE

Year 2007

Ever notice how most big men – when they hit their 70s or 80s – either soften up with pot bellies, or shrivel – while a few keep their bulk, looking like tough old trees – all rough bark and solid limbs?

Boris Katinsky is one of those tough old trees.

"My granddaughter, she is missing, and you got to find her," are his opening words as he barges into my office.

The accent is Russian, I guess. But I don't care about that. All I'm interested in is, how this guy got past Rose Shapiro, my usually non-moveable, seventyish, secretary-telephone operator-receptionist-bookkeeper-researcher-Jewish   Mother-everything. Rose always stands solid as a Dutch dike between me and people who wander – or barge – into my office without an appointment.

To explain, I'm Will Jonas, a private security consultant. And in this business, I never know who might want to see me with some imagined, or maybe even a real, gripe. Rose usually manages to defuse, or at least delay those types, while alerting me via an inter-office buzzer.

Too much concern about security, you're thinking? Grab up any newspaper, friend, and read about some aggravated guy who shot his boss. Or an irate client who decides his lawyer doesn't deserve to live, after his lousy handling of his case.

As I said, I'm a private security consultant.

Is that like a private detective? A private investigator? A private eye?

Well, yes. But you know, nowadays marketing is everything. It's the sizzle that sells. At least, that's what I was told when I took that evening marketing course at Pierce Community College back in 1995, when I was about to retire from the Los Angeles Police Department. At the time, I was a detective first grade, Homicide, working in the San Fernando Valley.

Like most guys taking their twenty or thirty, I was too young for a rocker or a fishing pole. And I didn't play golf.

So what's an ex-cop to do?

Security work, of course.

But I wasn't about to put on a square shield and a uniform, and spend my nights with my partner-dog, checking out storage yards.

And no one was rushing up with offers for me to head the security department of some corporation.

But maybe most important, I was tired of working for someone else. Yes, I know that sounds oddball, coming from someone who spent thirty years working for the Department.

But there is one thing I learned from those thirty years, and it's what always got me into trouble with the by-the-book guys. I don't take orders very well. I like to do things my way – and – on my own.

And if I do say so myself, it's been a productive ten years since I started my agency. Sure, I had plenty of those hot sheet motel surveillance cases at first. But I concentrated on getting business assignments.

Companies that needed employee security checks.

Or who were smart enough to worry about how their financial people were handling their cash flow.

Or how much inventory might be going out the door, unaccounted for.

Now, most of my business is corporate related, so I'm certainly not interested in looking for this guy's granddaughter.

But, here he is, clomping toward my desk.

"You got to find my Nina," Mr. Russia demands.

Behind him, hidden by his bulk, is Rose. She'd tried to keep him out of my office, but at five feet two inches, she's no match for the guy.

I, on the other hand, am. I'm six four, weigh 210, and although I'm 65, I still work out regularly.

I stand up to meet the guy, eyes-to-eyes.

"Who are you?" I ask. "And for missing persons, you should go to the police."

"I go there. They got nothing good for me. I am Boris Katinsky. And I am needing your help. Please."

His face is full of a grandfather's pleading, as he reaches into his pocket and takes out an envelope.

"You got to help me. I can pay. I can pay good," he says, shoving the envelope toward me.

"Whoa. Hold on, Mr. Katinsky, let's slow things down here a little."

I motion to the chair on his side of my desk.

"Sit," I order.

He sits.

"Want some coffee? Water?"

"No. No. Not important."

I nod at Rose and she leaves.

I sit down in the chair on my side of the desk.

"Look, Mr. Katinsky, I don't know why you decided to come to me. But there are better ways to look for a missing person. Regular police procedures…"

"I know. I know," he cuts me off. "You got to wait 24 hours and then you report. But Paul and Natalia, they don't want to report, so the police say Nina is not missing. But I know she *is* missing. Almost two weeks, now."

"Who are Paul and Natalia? Her parents?"

"No. Her parents, they die in car accident, back in Russia. Paul and Natalia are her – how you say it – her sponsors. Paul is cousin. When Nina wants to come here, Paul and Natalia say she can be with them."

"So," I point out, "if she lives with them, they ought to know if she's missing, right?"

"Supposed to," he corrects me, "but she is living with Aleksi, now. That no good bastard. And he say, too, she not missing. Everyone lies! They all lie about my Nina!"

See why I like to do corporate work, and not this kind of personal, missing persons stuff? Boris has been in my office for what, five minutes – and I feel like I'm in the middle of *War and Peace*. Nina. Aleksi. Natalia. Paul. Boris.

Boris just keeps rolling.

"Detective Black. He tell me to come see you. He say you can help me."

Thank you, Charlie Black. Charlie was my partner back in Homicide. And whenever something comes across his desk that's not really police work, Charlie steers it to me.

"You got to help me," Boris pleads.

Despite his roughness, there is something about this guy that I like. Maybe it's his directness. His no-bullshit approach.

I decide to see if I can help him. I take out a fresh note pad from a drawer in my desk.

"Okay," I say to Boris, "let's get some details here."

"What you want to know?" he asks. He leans forward eagerly. "We in business together?"

Well – not exactly the way I would put it. But what the hell.

"Yeah. We in business together."

CHAPTER TWO

The details are pretty simple, as Boris tells them to me.

"I come here, to America, and Los Angeles, seven years ago. No children. My wife, she die. Many years ago. Back in Russia."

"Paul and Natalia?" I prompt.

"They come maybe a year after me. From the same place in Russia. Part of family. But not real – how you say it – not real close." He shrugs. "But we sometimes friendly here. Family is family, right?"

"And Nina?"

Boris's face lights up.

"Ah, Nina. You know, her real name is Eugenia. But she get here, and she want to be American, all the way. So, she pick Nina."

"When was that?"

"When was what? When she pick Nina? I told you. When she get here."

"And when, exactly, did she get here?" I ask, wondering if I really want to do this.

"My Nina, she come to Los Angeles two years ago." Boris pauses, then smiles. "Happiest time for me."

"You two get along?"

"I love my Nina," Boris says strongly. "And she love me. We spend lots of time together, when she come here."

Then his face clouds over.

"Until Aleksi," he says. "That bastard!"

Well, one thing I could see. I didn't know yet what Aleksi's last name was, but "bastard" seems to be a part of it, as far as Boris is concerned.

"Who is Aleksi? What's his last name?"

"Aleksi Kaledin."

"And he's who Nina moved in with?"

"Six months ago." Boris slams his fist down on my desk. "And ever since, I don't see so much of Nina."

I guess I shook my head just enough so Boris caught it.

"What's the matter? What you thinking?" he demands. Then he answers his own questions. "You think maybe I'm like some crazy old grandfather that don't know Nina needs a young man? That when she find him, I see her not so much?"

"Well..." I begin. I shouldn't have bothered. Boris is on a roll.

"I know all that. And for the right man, I am happy for Nina. Even for her to move in with him." He shrugs. "Even that. Times change. I know." He shakes his head. "But not Aleksi. He is wrong for Nina. He is wrong for anyone. He is a gangster!"

I wonder if "gangster" is replacing "bastard" as Boris's favorite descriptive word for Aleksi? Or if Boris means that Aleksi is on the wrong side of the law? So I ask.

"What do you mean by gangster?"

"I mean bad guy! Wise guy! Russian Mafia!"

Well, I could see that Boris did know all the right terms from the cop shows, but I want something more specific, so I ask, "Do you know if this Aleksi has ever been arrested?"

Boris gets a bit defensive.

"No, I don't think he ever been arrested."

But then he takes off again.

"But I know he is gangster. A hooligan! And when you go to see him, you will know, too!"

Got to hand it to Boris. He's the client, and here he is, telling me who I have to go see. But I decide to ignore that, because he is right. Aleksi is someone I do have to see.

I ask Boris, "Have you been to see Aleksi? To ask him about Nina?"

"Sure! You bet! But he say, she not missing. So I ask him, where is she? I don't see my Nina nowhere in your place. He tell me, she move out. They not together anymore, he say to me. They break up, he say. Maybe one, two months ago. And he don't know where she gone. He don't know anything!"

I summarize what I've learned so far.

"So, Paul and Natalia...and Aleksi...all say Nina isn't missing. But you say she is. Tell me something...could they be right? And you're wrong? Could it be that Nina wanted to go somewhere…on her own? Didn't want to see any of you right now? Maybe she had a tough breakup with Aleksi. And she just wants to get away from everyone for a while. Could that be?"

"No! Cannot be this!" Boris says, hitting the desk with his fist. "If she have problems, she would come to me! I am sure!"

Rose comes into the office.

"I thought you might want something to drink?" she asks, looking at both Boris and me.

I should tell you two things about Rose.

First, she runs everything for me in the office. For what I need, she's perfect.

Second, Rose has more curiosity than an encyclopedia editor, so I know she's wondering what Boris and I are talking about.

I make the introductions.

"Boris Katinsky, this is Rose Shapiro. Rose is my right hand. Everything I know, she knows."

I take the next couple of minutes to fill Rose in. When I finish, she smiles, satisfied, and asks her question again.

"Anyone want anything to drink?"

I shake my head and look over at Boris.

He's staring at Rose.

"You a good-looking woman," he announces.

Hey! What the hell is this? Old hormones waking up and going wild in my office?

But Rose doesn't seem to mind. I think it might be the first time someone's told her she's good looking since her husband died, twelve years ago.

"Thank you," Rose says to Boris – in a soft voice – one that I've never heard before.

"Can we get on with our discussion?" I ask.

Yeah, I know I sound a little irritated, but I want to get this investigation going. And if Boris and Rose want to exchange meaningful looks, they can do it on their own time.

Rose understands me well enough to know when to leave, and she does. I have Boris's full attention again. The hormones seem to be settling.

"What I need from you now," I tell him, "are the following. First, everything you can tell me about Nina. What she looks like, where she works or worked, where she used to hang out – and I assume you have a picture of her?

"Second, I need an address for Paul and Natalia. And tell me all you can about them.

"And third, where can I find Aleksi?"

CHAPTER THREE

To start my investigation, I decide to look for Nina at the end of the line…that is, at the coroner's office.

Nothing Boris told me has led me to think that Nina Golchek – that was the name Boris gave me for his granddaughter – might be dead. But I figured I might as well eliminate that possibility, since it was an easy one to check out.

Before going to the coroner's office the next morning, I call ahead and speak to an Officer Brian. It takes me about ten seconds to realize that Brian is one of those people, nearing the end of his time on the Job, who doesn't move his ass for anyone, or anything. He is on a perpetual coffee break.

So when I get to Brian's cubicle, I'm not surprised when he hands me a stack of pictures and says, "You wanted me to sort them out for you, get rid of the obvious wrong ones, but I didn't have the time."

He passes over the stack.

"You'll have to sort them," he says.

Sure. Like I couldn't figure that out for myself. Thank you, Officer Brian.

Leaving the man to dream about dancing doughnuts, I sit down at a nearby table and take out the picture of Nina that Boris had given me. In the shot, Nina comes across as pretty. Her face has Slavic, high-cheek-boned, angular features. She has large doe eyes, and her brown hair is cut short.

I put Nina's picture off to one side of the table and spread out Brian's photos.

My first pass is a quick look to eliminate the obvious. Kids, older women, ethnic minorities.

That leaves me with nine possibilities – and I study these more closely.

I'm relieved.

No Nina.

Sure, if I had found Nina among the Janes, it would have been a fast conclusion of the investigation.

But I didn't relish the idea of telling Boris that Nina was dead. It wasn't something I wanted to visit on the old guy.

I bring the stack of pictures back to Brian.

"Anything?" he asks, looking up from some report he is making believe he is reading.

"No. And I guess that's a good thing."

"Usually is," he agrees.

Brian nods at the shot of Nina that I'm holding.

"That who you're looking for?"

"Yes."

I hand the picture to Brian and he studies it.

"You know, I think I seen a picture of this girl before."

My stomach gives a little lurch.

"You mean, in another one of your files?"

"Nah. I mean, someone came in a week or two ago, with a picture of a girl looked like this. Also wanted to check against the Janes."

I'm surprised. I thought no one had filed a missing person's report with LAPD.

"Someone from Missing Persons?" I ask Brian.

"No, a civie," he answers.

`Interesting. If Boris had been in here already, and hadn't told me about it, I'd butcher him. Either I do the investigation my way, or I don't do it at all.

"What'd he look like?" I ask. "Old guy? He give you a name?"

Brian shrugs.

"I don't remember."

He shakes his head.

"Hey, I get a lot of people coming in here. Lots of stuff across this desk. I can't remember all of the details. Just that the picture looks familiar, you know what I mean?"

End of the road with Officer Brian.

Whoever had come in would remain a mystery for now.

Unless it was Boris? I need to check with him.

CHAPTER FOUR

When I get back to the office, who do I find?

Rose, of course, and that's no surprise.

But Boris is there, too, and he's bent over, close to Rose, while they look at something on her desk.

Wily old guy, that Boris. Watch out, Rose. Boris's hormones are up and moving again. And from the looks of her, I think Rose's might be stirring a bit, too.

They both look up when I come in – Rose a little flustered.

"Boris was showing me a picture of Nina," she says quickly, as Boris steps back a bit.

"Which reminds me," I say to Boris, "why didn't you tell me you went to the coroner's office?"

Boris is puzzled.

"I know what you mean."

Then it hits him, and he turns pale.

"You think Nina is dead? No! That cannot be!"

Yeah, I know I was kind of stupid – the way I sprang it on him.

"I'm sorry," I apologize. "No! She's not dead. That's just one of the steps I have to take. One of the places I have to check out."

It takes Boris a few beats to overcome the jolt, but that tough old bird does.

"It's okay," he says. "I understand you got to do certain things. But I sure don't want it to be that one."

Then he changes subjects.

"I been thinking about what you asked me. You know. About where maybe Nina went."

"And…?"

"And I think maybe San Francisco."

"Why San Francisco?"

"Because I take her there. Two, three times. She always like it very much. We have good time there. She say to me, 'Grandpa, I really like this place.' So, maybe she go there. You got to check that out, for sure."

There he goes, giving me orders again. Like, I have to check out San Francisco. Hey, why not? Only three quarters of a million people living up there. Nothing to it.

"Yeah, I'll be getting to that," I assure Boris.

I turn to Rose.

"Anything doing that I have to know about? Any calls I need to return?"

"Nothing that can't wait," she tells me.

She smiles at Boris, then looks at me.

"If it's all right with you, Boris wants to take me to lunch."

Is it all right with me? Rose never asked my permission before. Good going, Boris!

"Of course," I agree.

Could I do otherwise?

CHAPTER FIVE

On my list of people to see, as part of my investigation, are Nina's sponsors – Paul and Natalia – and the ex-boyfriend, Aleksi.

But before seeing them, I want more information, especially about Aleksi, and Boris's claim that he is a gangster, bad guy, wise guy, Russian Mafia – take your pick.

I call my ex-partner and still LAPD Homicide detective, Charlie Black. The guy who started all this by sending Boris Katinsky to me.

"Homicide, Detective Black," Charlie answers.

"I'm not sure if I should thank you or swear at you," I say.

Charlie laughs.

"Isn't that Boris something? We should have his balls when we get to his age."

"He's got them," I agree. "But next time, please direct him – and his balls – to somebody else, okay?"

"Huh! A couple of corporate clients and you're all big time."

"Yeah, everything goes to my head, I know, and that's why I agreed to take Boris on. To remind myself why I was put on this earth. To help out the" – and I purposely use this next word – " trodden."

It gets the reaction I want from Charlie.

"I think you mean, 'downtrodden,'" he says.

Gotcha, Charlie!

I quickly say, "You take trodden in whatever direction you want, and I'll trod where I want."

Was this an exciting conversation? I decide to bring it back to reality.

"Charlie," I ask, "who can I talk to in Organized Crime? I want to check out a guy that Boris says his granddaughter was living with. Boris says he's a gangster."

"A gangster?" Charlie latches onto the word. "Haven't heard that one much since the days of J. Edgar."

"Well, that was just one of the words Boris used to describe the guy. He also called him a bastard, a wise guy, a bad guy, and Russian Mafia."

"If it's Russian Mafia, you want to talk with Ray Malik. He's the resident expert. Even speaks the language."

"Can you smooth the way, before I give him a call?" I ask.

"Does a bear shit in the woods? I'll talk to him in a couple of hours. Now, I'm going into a meeting."

Charlie hangs up.

"Does a bear shit in the woods?"

When Charlie and I first started partnering, I used to go crazy when he'd give me answers like that. It took me a while to figure out that Charlie was a crossword puzzle-anagram-don't-give-a-straight-answer kind of guy. But once I learned the signals, the figuring was over.

Yeah. Not to worry. Bears *do* shit you-know-where, and Charlie *will* call Ray Malik.

CHAPTER SIX

When I arrive home that evening, my wife, Lu, greets me with a kiss and my usual drink – club soda on the rocks.

I'm sure you recognize that telltale sign. Yes, I'm a recovering alcoholic. Been sober now for almost 12 years.

I don't make a big deal about my addiction. It's always with me, but for many years now, all I need to control it is a meeting once in a while. The last one I went to was about six months ago.

This kiss-and-club-soda greeting is something Lu and I have been doing ever since we've been married, which is three years.

Second marriage for both of us. My first wife, Vera, had died three years before Lu and I met. And Lu had been single for about a year. She'd gone through a mess of a divorce, but there were no children, so that made the split easier.

We met when I was taking an evening beginner's computer course at Cal State Northridge. Lu was the instructor. During the day, she's the chief computer programmer for a California bank headquartered in Glendale.

Back to the present.

After kissing Lu and taking a sip of my drink, I ask, "What's for dinner?"

The same question millions of husbands ask every night when they arrive home, right?

Yes, but with Lu, that question has a special meaning.

To explain, a couple of years ago, Lu complained that "We're eating out too much. I'm getting tired of it. And the same goes for the home delivery or takeout meals we've been eating."

"But Lu," I pointed out, "all that you can make in the kitchen are hard-boiled eggs. And I'm only good at making scrambled eggs. So how can we eat more at home?"

"Easy," Lu assured me. "I'll take cooking lessons."

The thing you have to know about Lu is this. When she says she's going to do something, she does it – all the way. So, six months after her first cooking lesson, Lu was serving great – and I do mean great – meals. French, Italian, whatever. Eating at home is now a real treat.

Tonight, over coffee, after a great veal parmesan, I tell Lu about my new client, Boris – and his maybe-she's-disappeared-maybe-she-hasn't granddaughter.

And – about Boris's move on Rose – and her reactions.

"Well, why not?" Lu asks. "Rose may be in her 70s, but she's a lively one. No reason why she can't have a relationship. Her husband's been dead for what – more than 12 years? Time to move on, if she feels like it."

"Yeah, I agree. But I wonder if Rose's getting involved with Boris will have any effect on Melanie."

Who is Melanie, you ask?

Well, about a year ago, Melanie was a 12-year-old girl who suddenly was left without parents, when her addicted, battered, and abused mother killed the girl's alcoholic father and then committed suicide.

I'd met Melanie a couple of times, when I'd come to their home to question her father during a homicide investigation. I could see the family was dysfunctional as hell, and I felt bad for the girl as I watched her trying to cope with the situation. I left her my card, and told her if she ever needed anything, to call me.

It wasn't too long after that, when Melanie did call, asking for help. It was early evening, and right after her mother killed her father and then herself.

Fortunately, I was still in the office, and so was Rose.

We drove to Melanie's home in Junction City, a small city near the Port of Los Angeles.

As soon as Rose saw Melanie, she did a Jewish Mother, protective wraparound of the girl. And she hasn't let go since.

Rose applied to Family Services to become Melanie's guardian, but she hit a snag when Family Services decided Rose was too old to be a guardian. So Lu and I signed on as co-guardians – and since that time, everything has worked out well.

Melanie has – as they say – blossomed in her new and very loving environment. Usually she lives with Rose weekdays, and weekends with us, plus there are plenty of times when we are all together.

Now, back to the discussion Lu and I were having.

"You going to take up with someone, 10 years after I'm gone?" I tease.

There is validity to my question, of course. I'm 65 and Lu is 46. Like the insurance people would point out, based on their actuarial charts, Lu is almost certain to outlive me.

"I might not even wait 10 years," Lu says. "Don't want to miss out on too many of the good things that are around."

Looking at Lu, I know that if that time came, she'd have no problem attracting plenty of men. Lu may be 46, but she looks 10 years younger. She has deep red hair that goes with her maiden Irish surname – McClelland. She weighs about 130 pounds and is five feet nine inches tall. And she has that angular model's face with the high cheek bones and the perfect nose.

I put down my coffee cup and give my stomach an exaggerated pat.

"Well, that dinner took care of one of my needs," I say.

Lu gets the message.

"First, you clean up the dishes," she says. "Then we can consider your other needs."

CHAPTER SEVEN

She watched the bug crawl across the dirty window, from the lower right corner to the upper left.

What, she wondered, was the bug going to do when it reached that upper left corner? Where would it go next?

That was her problem, too, wasn't it? Where to go next?

Nina Golchek turned away from the window and burrowed deeper into the lumpy mattress, pulling the thin blanket up tightly across her shoulders.

She'd have to move again. Move and change her job. Another cheap room. Another low-end diner where the owner didn't push too hard for job history and experience, as long as he could squeeze her ass every once in a while.

She wondered how much longer she could keep running and hiding from Aleksi. As she had been doing, ever since she looked on his computer and saw how deeply he was involved in the Russian Mafia.

Maybe – then – she should have gone directly to the police?

Only she was afraid. Afraid they wouldn't be able to protect her. And her grandfather.

So, instead, she decided it would be best just to get away from him.

But in so doing – she could see now – she'd just gotten herself into an even worse mess.

She thought back to when she first met Aleksi.

She had immediately been attracted to him.

He was good-looking. And he seemed to be a successful businessman, a Russian émigré who had adapted well to the American way of life.

And although she wasn't aware of it at the time, Aleski, who at 35, was 13 years older than she, had quickly become the dominant one in their relationship, taming her normally independent nature.

So when, a few weeks after they met, he asked her to move in with him, she did, despite her grandfather's concerns.

It didn't take long, though, for her to realize that Aleksi's business interests weren't what they looked like from the outside. And she thought, then, about moving out.

But she hadn't. She had thought she loved him too much to leave. And she had deluded herself, too, into thinking that she could change him.

She was wrong on both counts. Soon enough, she realized there was no love, just her initial attraction to his looks and sophistication. While on his part, Aleksi treated her as an adornment. Like a new suit. Or a new car.

Aleksi owned her. She found that out, when she did finally say to him that she thought it would be best if she left. If she moved out.

Now, she shuddered as she recalled that time.

They were in bed, after they'd had sex. She no longer took any joy in the act. But she had feigned her orgasm, wanting to please him, hoping to put him in a good mood.

It was in the aftermath of their lovemaking, that she told him she thought it best if they separated. If she left.

"You're not leaving," he told her. "No woman leaves me. And if you try, then your grandfather, Boris, will pay the price."

He moved his hand across his throat in an unmistakable gesture.

Then, he settled down on his side of the bed and went to sleep, seemingly not at all bothered by what he had just said to her.

The next weeks were hell. She didn't know what she could do. How could she safely get away from him? And keep her grandfather safe, too?

Aleksi couldn't have cared less. He continued to treat her as he had before, as an adornment in public, and in private, as an object to satisfy him sexually.

Then, one day, there was an opportunity, when Aleksi was out.

Nina had her own computer, which Aleksi had bought for her when she moved in. She used it to play video games and other such trivia.

But this day, her computer crashed. Not usable.

Nina knew that Aleksi had his own computer, in his home office. But she also knew that Aleksi had told her never to use it.

However, Aleski had gone out, and had told her he had appointments that would keep him away for several hours.

So Nina went into his office. And to her surprise, she saw that Aleksi had not turned off his computer. Unusual. He always turned it off when he went out.

She decided there'd be no harm in using his computer, to play her video games. Just so long as she turned the computer off before his expected return.

But when she sat down at the computer to play her games, the temptation to look at the machine's contents was strong. So she opened a random file and began to read it. The file listed several stores and their owners, along with a percentage number for each store. She was surprised to see Paul and Natalia's names listed, next to that of their sporting goods store.

No indication, though, as to what the listing meant. But Nina sensed that the file, and probably other files on Aleski's computer, were connected to his criminal activities. And she realized that the file could be her way out. Her way of being able to leave Aleksi, with no harm coming to her grandfather – or to herself. She could hold the file over his head – bargaining with him to leave her and Boris alone, once she left him.

She had to copy the file!

But as she readied to do so, she heard the front door lock being engaged.   Aleksi was returning much sooner than she expected!

Nina barely had time to close the file, run from Aleksi's office to her room, and sit down in front of her computer, which is where Aleksi found her.

He came into her room. He didn't say anything at first. Just stood there.

Then, after several seconds, he asked, "You been here, in this room, all the time I been out?"

"Yes," she answered, "trying to fix my computer. It crashed."

"So...you've been here the whole time?"

"Yes."

Aleksi stared at Nina and she stared back, trying hard to look at him steadily, and not to show any concern.

Aleksi broke off his stare, turned, and left the room.

Nina heard him go next door to his office. After a moment, he called for her.

"Nina! Come here!"

She went into his office. He was seated at his desk, facing his computer.

He looked at her.

"You sure you didn't come in here?   And try and use my computer?"

"Of course not!" Nina hoped her answer sounded strong.

Aleksi continued to stare at her. The seconds went by. Then he shook his head from side to side.

"Don't ever use my computer," he warned. "Never. You understand?"

"I know that," she assured him. "You keep your computer locked, you told me," Nina said. "So I can't use it."

He continued to stare at her. Then he nodded his head toward the door.

"Okay...get out of here."

Trying to appear calm, Nina left Aleksi and returned to her room. She sat down and started thinking.

I've got to get away from him.

And we need to be protected. My grandfather and me.

For that, I need those records that I saw on his computer.

She shook her head.

I'm not going to have another chance to download them, though.

But I saw enough to tell the police. And to get them and the FBI to start going after Aleksi and his Russian Mafia people.

And to protect us!

A few days later, Nina had her chance.

Aleksi had gone out, telling Nina he wouldn't be back until late in the evening.

Once he was gone, Nina went to her closet, and reaching to the top shelf, she took down one of the purses stacked there. Opening it, she took out the money she had been saving from the frequent gifts Aleksi had given her in the earlier, better days of their relationship.

Almost three thousand dollars.

Enough to get her started. To get her away from him.

Then she wrote him a note.

She told him she was leaving, and she described enough of the file to convince him that she had read it.

She also told him she had made a copy of the file. This wasn't true, of course. Aleksi had returned too soon that day, for her to have done this.

But Aleksi didn't know this. And keeping up with this pretense, Nina warned him that she would go to the police with the file, if anything happened to her or her grandfather.

Then she left.

CHAPTER EIGHT

The top person on my want-to-see list is Aleksi Kaledin, since Nina was living with him when she disappeared.

I don't want to see Kaledin, though, until I have a better line on him – information I hope to get from Ray Malik, the Russian Mafia guru at LAPD.

Malik and I have been trading phone calls, but not connecting. So instead, I call someone else I want to talk with – Paul Andreyov. Boris had told me that Paul and his wife, Natalia, were Nina's sponsors when she came to the U.S.

I reach Andreyov at a phone number Boris gave me. It's at a sports and athletic equipment store in North Hollywood, in an area heavily settled by the latest wave of Russian immigrants.

Russians in Nikes. The American Dream.

For someone who is Nina's sponsor, Andreyov sure doesn't sound concerned about her. I have to push the guy to get him to agree to see me.

Finally, though, he says I should come to the store at seven this evening, when he and Natalia will be closing up. They'll be able to talk to me then.

When I reach "Paul's Sports & Athletic Equipment" store, I almost feel like I'm in Russia. Most of the stores on both sides of the street have Russian signs, more prominent than their accompanying English versions.

If an owner is supposed to be a mirror image of the business, then the Andreyov's flunk the test. Surrounded by displays of beautiful people camping outdoors, and muscled hunks in running and walking shoes, tennis sneakers, hiking shoes, climbing shoes – you name it – here is this thin, middle-aged couple, looking like they could use several steroid shots, legal or not.

Paul Andreyov lets me in, gives me a short, weak handshake, locks the door, and walks me halfway back in the store, where Natalia is waiting.

These Andreyovs' are not smilers. In fact, they both look as if their underwear is a few sizes too small.

"That Boris," Natalia greets me, her accent moderate and her English good, "he worries too much."

"I take that to mean you don't think Nina is missing?" I ask her.

Paul answers.

"No, we don't think Nina is missing."

"When's the last time you saw her?"

The Andreyov's exchange looks before Natalia answers.

"Maybe…only two weeks ago."

"Boris says she's been missing for a month," I tell her. "That's a lot longer than you're saying."

"What does Boris know?" Paul asks. "He's an old man."

Throughout this back and forth, I see the two of them looking at each other, and I get the feeling they have anticipated what I was going to ask them, and they've planned their answers accordingly.

Why would they do that, I wonder?

I decide to try the family approach, so I say to Paul, "You're Nina's cousin, right?"

"Yes…"

"So even if she's only been gone for a couple of weeks, aren't you worried? As family, as her sponsors, don't you think you should go to the police and report her missing?"

"No! No police!" Natalia says strongly, her face flushed. "We do not want the police involved. There is no need for it."

One of the things I realize I have to take into consideration is the fact that I am dealing here with Russians – people who have lived most of their lives in a police state. Maybe it isn't so strange that Natalia doesn't want to go to the police. Probably doesn't trust them. And I can understand that.

"Look, Mrs. Andreyov," I say, softening my tone, "I realize that in Russia, going to the police isn't something anyone likes to do. But it's different here. We have a better chance of finding Nina with the police involved in the search."

"No!" Paul shouts. "No police. We do not think Nina is missing," he tells me, Natalia nodding in agreement. "Nina goes places by herself, sometimes. That is what Aleksi tells us, too.

"He says, probably Nina just went somewhere alone for a while. He is not worried."

I ask, "Is that Aleksi Kaledin you're talking about?"

I was curious to see what they would say about Aleksi. So far, all I had were Boris's "bastard" and "gangster" labels to go by.

"Yes," Paul confirms. And then the two of them go at it again, exchanging glances. They both seem uptight at the mention of Aleksi's name.

"How do you know Aleksi?" I ask.

"Because Nina lives with him," is Natalia's quick and short reply.

I look at Paul. He is clearly the more nervous of the two of them. We stare at each other for a few seconds and then he speaks.

"Aleksi is a good fellow. He…helped us get this store. He even helps us now, with planning, and stock, and things…"

"Paul," Natalia interrupts him, "we got to go! Right now!"

Paul falls into line.

"Yes, we have to go," he mumbles.

I take out my card and hand it to him.

"I'd appreciate your letting me know, whenever Nina turns up. Or if you hear from her. Okay?"

Paul nods, takes my card and slips it into the breast pocket of his shirt. I'm sure he'll forget he has it, and I have visions of the card being reduced to pulp when the shirt is washed.

Ah well…

CHAPTER NINE

I leave the Andreyovs' with a puzzle to ponder, as I drive west on Ventura Boulevard, toward my office in Woodland Hills.

Boris says Nina has been gone for *four* weeks – and he is very concerned.

The Andreyovs' say Nina has been gone for only *two* weeks – and they aren't concerned.

Why the different calendars? And levels of concern? What is going on here?

And if this isn't enough to think about, now I discover what I suspect is a tail on me. A Ford Focus. Gray. Third car back. In my lane.

Can't be absolutely sure, so I decide to check it out. Going west on Ventura Boulevard, I come to Coldwater Canyon. I drive through it, switch over one lane, speed up and then check my mirror.

Sure enough, the tailing car cuts over to my lane and keeps up with me.

A few blocks later, I turn right, onto Van Nuys Boulevard, and look in the mirror. The Ford is right there.

I make a quick left onto Moorpark. The Ford makes the same turn, but drops back a couple more cars.

I decide I have three choices.

Choice #1 – lose the tail. I could do that, but why bother? By now, the person tailing me probably has run my plates and knows who I am. And by the way, it's not just law enforcement that can do that. Good hackers can get into the DMV system, too. He probably also knows where my office is, so if I lose him, he'll just stake it out and find me again.

Choice #2 – confront the tail. Hit the brakes, jump out of my car, pull my piece and shove it under his nose before he knows what is happening. Bad choice. Makes for good TV cop show action, but that's about it. Waving my gun at the guy could lead to all sorts of problems, with no good outcomes.

Choice #3 – don't do anything right now. Let him tag along. Then when I'm ready, maneuver him into a trap, where he's stuck and can't move. Then we can talk, and I can find out what the hell is going on.

Okay.

Decision made.

Time to get on the 101 Freeway and head back to my office, which I do at Sepulveda. Rose had told me I have a load of paperwork to check over, and that I better do it – and soon.

When Rose tells me to do something, I do it. The alternative isn't pretty.

Ah well, Super Sleuth by day. Management Drone by night. That's me.

CHAPTER TEN

"I got nothing on Aleksi Kaledin except a lot of suspicions."

That's what Ray Malik tells me when I meet him the next day, at the Country Deli on Lassen in Chatsworth. I'd offered to buy him lunch at the Deli, which was convenient to the police station on Devonshire in Northridge.

"What kind of suspicions?" I ask.

"Nothing you can go to the bank with. We know the guy's dirty. We just can't put it together, yet."

"How long you been trying?"

"Too damn long," Malik admits. "He is one very smooth guy. Not like most of the Russian Mafia types who bull ahead, and screw how it looks. Kaledin's more subtle. Works behind a front as a respectable businessman."

"What kind of business?"

"Got that big 'Futura Furniture' store in North Hollywood. Runs lots of teaser cable advertising. You know the type. Nothing down. Six months, no interest. Maybe you've seen it?"

I hadn't seen the advertising, but I had seen the store. It was on the same street where the Andreyovs' had their athletic shoe store.

"What do you think he's into?" I ask, "besides bedroom sets?"

"That's the ball buster," Malik says. "We keep trying to find some connection between him and the usual stuff. Drugs, protection, loan sharking, prostitution – but we come up empty."

Malik shifts subjects.

"Will, tell me more about why you're interested in Kaledin."

"It's like I said on the phone. My client claims his granddaughter's been missing for four weeks. She was living with Kaledin before that, so I want to ask him what he knows about it."

Malik shakes his head.

"Good luck, but you won't get anything Kaledin doesn't want to tell you. We've had him in a couple of times. To see if we could work anything out of him. Couldn't get anywhere. He's a tough nut."

Malik drums his fingers on the table and I know what's coming. Hey, I used to be a cop, remember?

"You know," he says, "if you punch any holes in that businessman front of his, and you let us in on what you learn, you'll be building up a lot of credit in the 'we owe you' bank. Good for any private investigator to have."

"Whatever I know, you'll know," I assure him.

Malik leans across the table, his face serious.

"Be careful, Jonas. The Russians are crude and cruel as hell. Kaledin comes across as smooth, but I wouldn't want to have my ass turned in his direction."

CHAPTER ELEVEN

So was it hard for me to see Kaledin?

No problem, thanks to good old Boris.

When I get back to the office, Rose gives me the news.

"Aleksi Kaledin says he will be in his store – Futura Furniture – all afternoon. So whenever you want to see him, he will be waiting for you."

She smiles at Boris, who is hovering near her desk – and I do mean hovering.

"Boris arranged it," she says, giving him another smile.

Definite lovebirds, Rose and Boris.

And as Lu would point out – why not?

"You going to see the bastard today, right?" Boris demands.

"Why, I'll just zoom over there right now," I assure him.

And so it is about an hour later, that I park my car in front of Futura Furniture, feed the meter and go into the store.

If Kaledin is Russian Mafia, and is using the store as a respectable front, then he is doing a good job of it. Futura Furniture is big, bright, and loaded with furniture displays in every direction.

Midway back in the store, in the dining room area, a tall, well-dressed man waves at me and walks quickly in my direction. As he nears, the man smiles and holds out his hand for me to shake.

"Mr. Jonas? Aleksi Kaledin. I've been expecting you. Welcome to Futura Furniture."

Kaledin has a Russian accent, muted by a well-modulated way of speaking. His voice, his body language, his clothing – all project sincerity and openness.

He's a few inches shorter than I am. Maybe six feet one or two, and a trim 180 or so pounds. He has a full head of dark brown hair, combed straight back. His face has all the required parts to it.

If I didn't know better, I'd easily take Kaledin for a successful furniture retailer, happy to help his customers pick out the right furniture for their dream homes.

I decide to go along with Kaledin's Chamber of Commerce image. No sense being hardnosed until, or if, necessary.

"Thanks for seeing me," I tell Kaledin, returning his handshake.

"Of course," Kaledin assures me. "If it is about Nina, of course I would see you."

He walks me to the back of the store and into his office. Closing the door, Kaledin motions me to a couch, where we both sit down.

"Can I get you anything?" he asks.

"Nothing," I tell him, "except information. About Nina. And where she is."

Kaledin shakes his head.

"Boris is a loving grandfather, but he worries too much."

"So you don't share his belief that Nina is missing?"

"No, I don't."

"When was the last time you saw her?"

"The day she moved out of my place. About four weeks ago."

I think, at least he and Boris agree on the timing.

I ask, "Doesn't it strike you as odd, that no one's seen or heard from her since? Maybe that's something to worry about?"

"No," Kaledin says. "Nina does things like that. She told me many times how she felt the need to get away from people, to be by herself for a while."

"So, you're not worried?"

Kaledin pauses before answering.

"Look, I wouldn't want Boris, or the Andreyovs', to hear what I'm going to tell you, so can we keep it between us?"

"Sure," I assure him. Anyway, my fingers are crossed behind my back.

"The truth is," Kaledin continues, "that even though I told you I'm not worried – well, I *am* beginning to get a little concerned. I'm pretty sure Nina's okay, but I'd feel better if I knew where she was. And I'd like to help you look for her."

I sure don't want to hook up with Kaledin in any joint search for Nina. But I sense that it might be useful to have him *believe* I welcome his help. Maybe it will give me a chance to do what Ray Malik wants. To get behind Kaledin's businessman front.

I tell him, "I usually work alone. But I appreciate your offer, and I'm sure there will be times when I could use your help. Can I turn to you, at those times?"

"Absolutely."

"Good. Now, there is one immediate way you can help me."

"What's that?"

"By answering some questions that I have."

"Okay. Fire away."

"First, why did Nina leave you?"

Kaledin shrugs.

"I wish I knew. She left one day, when I was out on business. No note. No anything."

"Any idea where she may have gone?"

"I've been thinking about that. She used to talk about how much she enjoyed visiting San Francisco with Boris. Maybe she's up there?"

"Boris thinks so, too," I tell him. "I'm planning on going up there."

"Maybe I can come along?" Kaledin suggests.

No, I decide, that would be going farther than I want to go, in the cooperation department.

"I'll do that one solo," I tell him.

"Okay. But what *can* I do to help out?"

"Why don't you work up a list of people that Nina knows. And some other places you think she might be. We can look at those lists, and split them up between us."

Now, I switch subjects, in order to probe a bit. I look around the store.

"Some place you have here," I say to Kaledin, in what I hope is an admiring tone. "Been in this business for a while?"

"For a while," he confirms.

"You look like the kind of businessman who might have some other things going, too," I push. "That so?"

Kaledin laughs.

"I'm just a furniture guy," he tells me. "No other business. This place keeps me busy."

Yeah, sure, I think. There's a lot more to this guy than dining room sets and king size beds. Malik's right about that, even though he hasn't been able to come up with anything.

And on my part, I have to wonder if Kaledin knows more about Nina and her four-week absence than he is letting on. It's a definite possibility.

I look around Kaledin's office and decide I need to pay it a private visit. At night, after the lights are out, Louise. It's called "Breaking and Entering," but it only counts if you're caught, and I don't intend to have that happen.

I've had enough of Aleksi Kaledin for the time being, so I stand up.

"That ought to do it for today," I tell him. "Thanks for your help."

Kaledin assures me, "I'll work on that list right away."

******

After Jonas leaves, Kaledin walks to his desk and sits down.

Things may be turning good now, he thinks. Maybe this Jonas guy will be able to find Nina.

Kaledin shakes his head.

Where the hell is she? He has several people out there, trying to find her, but no one has been able to do so.

Well, now this Will Jonas guy is searching, too. And he's good, based on his past reputation as a cop.

Kaledin nods.

Okay. I need to put some people on Jonas, as he does his search. And if he finds her, then I'll have them kill Jonas and bring Nina to me.

Once I can go to work on her, I'll get that damn file.

Kaledin smiles at his next thought.

Then I can kill Nina – and that pain-in-the-ass Boris, too.

CHAPTER TWELVE

As I drive away from Kaledin's store, there it is again. A car following me. Only this time, instead of a Ford Focus, it's a Chevrolet Malibu.

To make sure, I take a few left and right turns as I work my way over from Lankershim to Ventura Boulevard.

The Chevy stays with me.

But it's not a good tail. Yeah, the driver is making all the right moves, sometimes three cars behind, or moving over to another lane, then falling back four or five cars – trying to avoid setting a pattern that can be spotted.

Problem is, there should be two – or even better, three – cars in the operation. Much less likely to be discovered under those conditions.

So, okay, it isn't a high budget operation. But why a tail at all? Why is someone following me? And why was someone following me when I left the Andreyovs' store?

Time to get some answers.

By now, I'm on Ventura Boulevard, between Van Nuys and Sepulveda Boulevards. There's a Ralph's Supermarket a few blocks west of Van Nuys, and when I reach Ralph's, I turn right at the northeast corner, and then take an immediate right, into the underground parking garage. A short way in, I spot the kind of parking space that I want, and I turn right into it.

The Chevy follows me into the garage, passes where I'm parked, goes down a bit, and pulls into a space in the same line I'm in.

Perfect! Just what I hoped would happen.

I picked this parking line because the garage wall is right in front of it. So the only way out for any car in this parking line, is to back out. No driving forward.

I back my car out of my parking space – fast. Then I drive down to the space occupied by the tail. And I stop right behind it.

The tail is now trapped. Can't go forward. There's the wall. Can't back out. There's my car.

I look at the Chevy. Only one person in it. The driver.

I open my glove compartment, take out the Glock, put in a clip, make sure the safety is engaged, and put the weapon in my waistband, behind my right hip.

Now, I get out of my car and walk to the driver's side of the Chevy.

Staring up at me – and is she pissed – is an attractive woman. Looks to me like she's in her late 20s or early 30s.

I motion for her to roll down the window.

"Who are you?" I ask. "And why are you following me?"

She stares at me for a few seconds and then starts to reach for her handbag, on the passenger seat next to her.

"Don't do that!" I warn, making sure she sees me moving my right hand inside my jacket.

She stops – and instead, puts both her hands on the steering wheel.

"I'm Special Agent Dorothea Marquez, Federal Bureau of Investigation. And if you'll let me get my handbag, I'll show you my ID."

"Okay. But slowly and carefully."

She extends her right hand to the passenger seat, picks up the handbag, brings it over to her lap and opens it, with the opening tilted so I can see inside the bag.

No weapon.

She reaches into the bag, takes out a small leather pouch, opens it, and holds up her FBI identification.

I examine it. Looks real to me.

"Satisfied?" she asks.

I nod.

"Yeah, I'm satisfied that you're Special Agent Dorothea Marquez. But I'm not satisfied – and I don't like – that you're tailing me. Twice now. Why?"

Marquez doesn't immediately answer, and when she does, her voice reflects her anger.

"You going to take your hand away from your weapon? You're not going to shoot me, are you? That would be pretty stupid."

"Almost as stupid as the obvious tail you were running on me. You sure you're FBI? I thought they trained you better than that."

We stare at each other.

"So again, why are you tailing me?" I ask.

"It's... part of an investigation," Marquez answers.

"Gee, you could have fooled me. I thought maybe it was because you liked the way I look."

"I like them a lot younger," she comes back at me.

And then, nothing. No more words from her.

"Okay," I say, "I can play the 'silence game' too."

I turn and start walking toward the entrance to Ralph's.

"Hey!" Marquez shouts, scrambling out of her car. "You can't leave me like this."

I look at her as if I don't understand.

"Why not?" I ask.

She points toward her car.

"Because I can't get out."

"How about that?"

I stare at her. She stares at me. She breaks first.

"Okay, I'll tell you what I can. Then, will you move your car?"

"Talk," I order.

"We...we're investigating some things on that block. And when I saw you go into those two stores, and not buy anything, I wondered what your business might be with those places. So I decided to follow you."

"What? Window shopping is breaking the law? Because I didn't buy anything, you decide to follow me?"

"Can you drop the attitude, please? It's...well, I had my reasons. That's all I can say."

She's right about my attitude, so I drop it.

"Look," I tell her, "we got off on the wrong foot. Can we start over again?"

I give her a smile. She gives me a bit of a smile. Not much. But it's a beginning.

"Okay," I start up again, "you said you were investigating some things on that block. Like what? Who?"

"I can't say."

I look over at her car and shrug.

"Suit yourself."

I turn toward the Ralph's.

"Okay, okay," she concedes. "We're conducting a surveillance on the man you were seeing – Aleksi Kaledin."

I think about that. If the FBI is investigating Kaledin, that means they suspect he might be involved in something interstate. The Feebies don't bother with local goings on, unless there's a multi-state angle.

I wonder why Ray Malik at LAPD didn't mention any FBI investigation to me, when we talked. Of course, he didn't have to tell me. Could have decided it was none of my business.

I didn't think that was the reason, though. I think Malik didn't tell me about the FBI investigation – because he didn't know anything about it.

Wouldn't be the first time the FBI operated in a local jurisdiction without telling the local authorities. I knew this from my LAPD days.

I tell Agent Marquez, "Yesterday, I talked to the LAPD specialist on the Russian Mafia. And he didn't say anything about your investigation. I bet he doesn't know anything about it, right?"

Marquez doesn't say anything. Obviously, she doesn't want to answer my question.

"Look," I tell her, "I'm not trying to give you a hard time, but I don't like being followed. You going to call it off now?"

"Yes."

"And can we talk more about Kaledin? I've got some questions about him. Maybe you can give me some answers."

Marquez shakes her head.

"I… can't say much…"

"I promise I won't push. I just want to get more of a feel for the guy."

"Well…okay."

"Great. But first, let me go move my car. Then, there's a coffee bar in Ralph's. Why don't you go ahead, and I'll meet you in there. My treat."

I catch her looking at the wedding band on the ring finger of my left hand.

"Hey, I'm not making a move on you. I am very, and I mean, very happily married. And anyway, like you said before, I'm too old for you."

Marquez laughs.

"Okay. I'll be in the coffee bar."

CHAPTER THIRTEEN

In the coffee bar, we get our coffees, and go through the formalities, so that she's Dorothea and I'm Will.

Dorothea is Latina. About five feet five inches. Tightly built, with broad shoulders and a compact frame. Her black hair is cut short. Her face is attractive. Large brown eyes. A killer smile, when she relaxes.

I ask the first question.

"Why are you looking at Kaledin?"

Dorothea takes her time answering, obviously deciding what she will tell me.

"The FBI is conducting a national investigation of the Russian Mafia. What areas of crime they're into – or getting into. How they are doing so. How they connect around the country. Kaledin's name has started to come up as part of this investigation. So we're taking a closer look at him."

"But how does that tie in to your tailing me?"

Dorothea shakes her head.

"What I'm going to tell you now is – well, it's kind of embarrassing. So I hope you won't laugh too much."

I raise my coffee cup.

"I promise."

"Okay. So, I called up your creds, while you were in that sporting goods store – just down the block from Futura Furniture. Saw your background. Impressive."

She paused.

"Now, here comes the embarrassing part. The stakeout of Kaledin was boring...boring...boring. I decided I needed a little break from it. So when you left that sporting goods store – and also when you left Kaledin – I figured I'd try tailing you, to see how good you were at spotting a tail. And how good I was, at avoiding detection. And how good I was at staying with you, if you did spot me and tried to lose me."

She shakes her head.

"But the tail was really a dumb idea, on my part."

"Not too bright," I agree with her. "But hey, I've got too many years of experience on you, for you to ever beat me in a tailing contest."

"What do you mean? Despite how hard you tried, you couldn't shake me. Either time."

"Yeah, but still – you lost."

"How so?"

"May I remind you of what happened in the parking garage?"

She laughs. "Okay, you win."

She grows serious.

"All right, now *I* need some answers, please, Will."

"Like what?"

"Like, what are you doing with a lowlife like Kaledin?"

"I have a client – a grandfather – who thinks his granddaughter is missing. She was living with Kaledin until four weeks ago, when she disappeared. And I'm trying to find her."

"What do the police say?"

"Nothing. Because the girl's sponsors – the girl is Russian and came over here a few years ago – they haven't filed a missing person's report. They think she's just off somewhere, on her own, having a good time."

"But the grandfather thinks differently?"

"Right. And that's why I went to see Kaledin. To find out what he knows."

"Did you learn anything useful?"

"Nothing. Kaledin says her leaving was a surprise to him. She didn't leave him a note. Nothing. And he hasn't heard from her."

"And you believe him?" Dorothea asks, her disbelief obvious.

I smile at her.

"Dorothea, how can you be so cynical at your tender age?"

Chapter Fourteen

Nina's hands were still shaking, even though it was hours since she had seen Pyeter Golnikov, one of Aleksi's men.

It was when she was walking to her newest job, a coffee shop where she had been working only a week. She spotted Golnikov as he came out of the restaurant. Luckily for her, Golnikov was looking in the opposite direction.

Nina ducked into a shop doorway.

`The shaking began as Golnikov turned and looked in her direction. He didn't see her, though, and he went back into the restaurant.

Well, for certain, she couldn't go back to that job. Not now. Not ever.

She waited to see if Golnikov came out again. When he didn't, Nina left her hiding place and began walking quickly toward her apartment.

When she arrived on the block where she was living – in a shabby, one-room unit, cash in advance, not using her real name, of course – she walked slowly and carefully toward the building, checking for any more of Aleksi's men.

She didn't see anyone. Hopefully, they hadn't yet discovered where she was living. She had given a false address to the coffee shop owner.

She reached the building, went to her second floor apartment, let herself in, and locked the door.

But turning the lock didn't make her feel safe! Instead, she was panicked by the realization that Aleksi was close. So close!

She tried to calm herself, as she sat down and thought about what to do.

Obviously, the job at that diner, her third since arriving in San Francisco, was over. No great loss. She'd be able to find another one.

But if Aleksi's people were in San Francisco looking for her, it was going to become increasingly difficult to stay hidden from him.

She touched her hair and face. She had done all she could to change her appearance. Her dark brown hair was now blond, and styled differently.

She had used makeup more heavily than was her custom, with an emphasis on fuller, redder lips and heavy eye shadow.

Aleksi's men would recognize her in person, but it was possible that someone looking at a picture of her, might not.

Nina looked around her one-room unit. No doubt, Aleksi was having his men check places like this. Cheap, by-the-week lodgings.

She'd better move again.

She began gathering up her few belongings. The room was paid up for two more days, but that couldn't be helped.

As she packed, Nina knew that in addition to renting another apartment and getting a new job, there was something else she had to do. She needed to get a message to Aleksi. She must convince him that he'd better stop trying to find her. Or else she would go to the police.

She wanted to emphasize to him again, just as she had in her note, that if he left her and her grandfather alone, she'd remain silent.

But Aleksi wasn't leaving her alone. He was doing just the opposite. He was looking for her.

Well, she had to reinforce her message! Try to make him believe it!

So? How to do this? How to convince Aleksi to stop searching for her?

She worried about how to deliver this message to Aleksi. If she called him, she didn't trust herself to be strong enough – even on the telephone – to convince him. He frightened her so!

She thought about calling her grandfather and having him deliver the message.

No, that wouldn't do. Aleksi had threatened to kill Boris. And if now, Boris came to Aleksi with a message from her – well, there was no telling what Aleksi might do.

Then, who else?

Why not Paul Andreyov? He and Natalia were Nina's sponsors, so it would be natural for Nina to communicate with Aleksi – through them.

******

Several hours later, in the evening, Nina left the new apartment she had just rented. She walked a few blocks until she found a public telephone. They were getting harder and harder to find.

She called the Andreyovs, expecting they'd be home from their store by now.   Paul answered, and Nina spoke to him, their conversation in Russian.

"Paul? Hello. This is Nina."

"Nina! Where are you?"

"I can't say, Paul, but I'm all right."

"What's going on, Nina? Why did you go away?"

"It's very complicated, Paul.   And I really can't explain everything.   But I need your help.   I need you to talk to Aleksi Kaledin."

At the mention of Kaledin's name, Paul stiffened.

"What...what do you mean? Talk to Aleksi Kaledin?"

"I want you to deliver a message to him from me."

"Why can't you call him yourself, Nina? I'm sure he would like to hear from you."

Nina laughed harshly. She bet Aleksi would!

To Paul, she said, "There are reasons why I can't do it myself. Please, Paul. I need you to do it."

"All right," he agreed reluctantly.   "What...what is the message?"

"Tell Aleksi to stop looking for me. Or else."

There was a pause, until Paul spoke, his concern clear.

"What...what does this message mean, Nina? Why is Aleksi looking for you? And what does – 'or else' – mean? This worries me – this message you want me to give to Aleksi."

"Paul, believe me, the less you know, the better. Just give Aleksi the message. Will you do that for me?"

Paul sighed.

"All right. I...will do it."

"Soon? It's important to tell him soon!"

`"Yes, yes, soon," Paul assured her.

"Now tell me, Nina, where are you? When are you coming back? Boris keeps telling us we should file a missing person's report with the police. But we have not done so. Aleksi thinks you probably are just off somewhere, wanting to be alone, after you decided to leave him. So, we have not filed a report."

What Paul is telling Nina confirms her worst fears. Aleksi wants to find her on his own. He doesn't want the police to be looking for her. Afraid of what she might tell them, if they get to her first.

"I can't say any more right now," Nina says to Paul, in response to his question. "I just need you to do what I asked you. Do you promise?"

"Yes, I promise. But Nina..." Paul stops talking as he hears the click, as Nina breaks the connection.

CHAPTER FOURTEEN

Paul hangs up the phone, and Natalia, who has been listening to his end of the conversation, peppers him with questions.

"What did Nina say? Where is she? What is it you promised?"

Paul shakes his head.

"Nina said I should not tell anyone where she is. And I should give her message only to Aleksi.

"This is getting more and more difficult," Paul says to his wife, the concern clear in his voice. "It is not what I expected when we first agreed to go ahead with Aleksi."

Natalia looks at Paul, almost coldly.

"We knew the price to pay," she reminds him.

"I know," Paul admits. "But this business with Nina, it has me worried. Aleksi won't say why she went away. And now, she calls and she won't tell me anything. And she wants me to give a message to Aleksi. What is this…'or else?' I tell you, Natalia, this whole business concerns me."

"You have to keep your nose out of it, Paul," Natalia urges. "Just give Aleksi the message, and that's all. Don't ask him questions."

"But, Natalia, I am responsible for Nina. *We* are responsible for her. We are her sponsors."

"We have done our duty," Natalia answers. "We brought Nina here. We took care of her. She is the one who moved out, to go live with Aleksi. She is an adult. It is her business!"

"This is family!" Paul protests.

He pauses, takes a deep breath and stands up.

"I am going to see Aleksi."

"Only to deliver the message," Natalia cautions.

Paul nods. "Yes. Only to deliver the message."

But he thinks to himself – and to get some answers.

CHAPTER FIFTEEN

When is Halloween?

The question pops into my mind, as I look at myself in the mirror, in my office bathroom.

What I see is me, in a Ninja-like outfit. Black everything – pants, shirt, socks, sneakers, and wool cap.

I look like a comic book character.

But hey, it's okay. It's what I need to wear, to do what I need to do.

Which is to break into Aleksi's office at Futura Furniture, and see what there is to see.

I check the time. 11 o'clock. Futura Furniture has been closed for two hours, since 9:00 p.m. Time to go.

Forty minutes later, I park my car around the corner from Futura Furniture. When I went to see Aleksi Kaledin, I'd seen a driveway to the right of the building. Now, I use that driveway to get to the back of Futura.

There's a door next to the shipping and receiving dock. I check the lock. It doesn't look serious, and it isn't. A few minutes with my burglar set, and the lock is conquered.

Once inside the store, I see lights that have been left on to highlight some of the furniture for window shoppers.

I avoid those, and walk to Aleksi's office. The door is locked, but my burglar set does me proud again.

I look around the office and go to Aleksi's desk. Good place to start, to look for whatever the hell it is I'm looking for. Lousy sentence structure, but you know what I mean.

I go through the papers on his desk. Nothing unusual. Same with what's in the desk drawers.

There's a four-drawer metal cabinet in one of the corners, and I make that the next project for my burglar set. Success once again!

I look through the files in the first three drawers. Nothing of interest. Just catalogs, shipping and receiving documents, bills of sale, that kind of stuff.

But in the bottom drawer, I find something in the first file that I open.

It's a sketch of the street where Futura is located. Futura is shown on that sketch, but the sketch also has all the other stores on the block, including the Andreyovs'.

Some of the stores have check marks. Others don't.

I wonder what that means.

I examine the sketch, looking for an explanatory legend, like they have on maps and blueprints. But there's nothing.

Well, maybe the next file will give me some more information?

I bend down to pick out that file, when I hear a sound I don't want to hear.

Police sirens. And they're coming fast.

What the hell!

I'd checked for an alarm when I came in, but didn't find any. I must have missed the damn thing.

Okay. I need to get the hell out of here before the police arrive.

One good thing – I'm wearing gloves, so I don't need to worry about my fingerprints showing up.

I put the file with the sketch back in the bottom drawer and slam the drawer shut. I run across the office to the exit door, push the lock button from the inside, come out of the office and close the door.

Now I go back to the door where I first came in. I open it a few inches and look out. No one out there.

I push the interior button for the lock, step outside, and close the door.

I hear tires squeal out front as some police cars pull up. My heart starts pounding and I remember what Robert Redford said in one of his movies a few years back. What was the name of it? *Sneakers,* I think. What he said was, "I'm getting too old for this."

Correct, Robert!

"Hey, Stupid," I address myself – "get your sorry ass moving!"

Taking my own advice, I run down the alley, but not in the direction from where I'd originally come. Instead, I head in the other direction. This puts me on the block behind Futura Furniture, where I turn right, and run to the first corner, then right again, to my car.

I get in and start the engine, as ahead of me at the intersection I see a couple of police cars speed through, and then I hear their tires protest as the drivers pull to a stop.

Not going to go that way! I jam my car in a hard u-turn and go in the opposite direction, checking my mirror to see if a police car might have spotted me. Nothing.

At the corner, I turn right and cut my speed back to thirty-five. No sense getting pulled over for speeding.

"And where were you going, Sir, at seventy miles an hour in a thirty-five-mile zone?"

"Well, Officer, I was just trying to get away from the scene of my crime."

No, it wouldn't do to get stopped.

A half hour later, I'm back in my office, taking off my Ninja outfit, when the phone rings. I think about not answering it, but decide I might as well. Couldn't have anything to do with what had just happened at Futura Furniture. The police wouldn't have called me about that. They'd have paid me a personal visit.

I pick up the phone.

"'Hello," I say, working to calm my voice, and doing a pretty good job of it, if I do say so myself.

"Find anything good at Futura Furniture? Perhaps just the bedroom set you've been looking for?"

It's Marquez. As in, FBI Agent Dorothea Marquez.

I don't know what to say. And I don't want to say something stupid, like, "I don't know what you're talking about."

Because, obviously, she *does* know what she's talking about.

At this point, I can only think of one thing to say, so I say it.

"Why don't you come over, so we can talk."

CHAPTER SIXTEEN

When I open the door for Marquez, she flashes me a "gotcha" grin.

"So, what about that bedroom set?" she asks.

I don't answer her.

"Come on," she teases, "Ninjas can talk."

I decide an offense is my best defense, so I come back with, "What are you doing following me again? Didn't you learn your lesson last time? Explain yourself."

Dorothea laughs.

"I think you have things turned around. I don't owe *you* an explanation. *I* wasn't breaking and entering."

She stares at me. I stare at her.

But let's face it. She's right. I *was* committing a crime at Futura.

I soften my attitude.

"Okay, obviously, you're not turning me in. Why?"

Dorothea smiles.

"Well, I figure if Ninja finds anything of interest, I just know he'll be willing to share it with me."

The lady has me firmly gripped. And I know it.

"In other words, it's okay for me to break and enter, just so long as I share with you anything I find that will be useful to your investigation. Do I have that right?"

She smiles again.

"You are one bright Ninja."

Dorothea turns serious.

"Will, I'm not trying to give you a hard time. But your sharing with me may be helpful."

I nod.

"Okay. Fair enough."

I take a minute to organize my thoughts.

"As I told you before, when I met with Kaledin, I thought he was holding out on me. Not telling me everything about Nina and her disappearance. And that's why I did my B&E tonight. To see if there was anything in his office that might help me."

"And did you find anything?"

"No, nothing about Nina. But I did find something interesting – although I'm not sure what it means."

"What's that?" Dorothea asks.

"In one of Kaledin's files, there was a sketch, a drawing, with all of the stores on the block in it. Some of the stores had check marks on them, but others didn't. But there was no information on the sketch as to what it all means.

"I was about to go through more files, to see if I could find something explaining the sketch, but then I heard the sirens."

I shake my head.

"How the hell did I miss that alarm, when I went in?"

Dorothea has a puzzled expression on her face.

"Will – about the sirens – you don't know what happened? You didn't hear anything on the police band? Or on the all-news radio station?"

"What are you talking about? Hey, I was kind of occupied with getting away from the scene of my crime."

"Will, you didn't trip any alarm at Futura. The police have no idea you were in there. The black and whites were going to another store – down at the end of the block – Paul's Sports & Athletic Equipment."

"I know that place. And the owner, Paul Andreyov."

"Past tense, Will. You *knew* him. Andreyov was killed tonight."

CHAPTER SEVENTEEN

On the one hand, what Dorothea tells me helps my ego. Okay. I'm not losing my touch. I didn't set off any alarm at Futura.

On the other hand – well – I don't have any other hand. I have no idea why Paul Andreyov was killed. So, being the trained investigator that I am, I ask questions.

"What happened?" (Am I brilliant?)

"I don't know much," Dorothea answers. "Remember, the police are not aware of the FBI's interest in Kaledin, or my surveillance of him. So I can't ask them any direct questions.

"What I *did* do, was join the crowd outside the store. And I listened as one of the TV reporters did her on-camera piece for the next news segment. She said the police discovered Andreyov's body in his store, after someone walking by noticed that the door was open. That person called the police."

I think back to my meeting with the Andreyovs.

I tell Dorothea, "I met with the Andreyovs, to talk about Nina's disappearance. And I could see that the wife, Natalia, didn't want to get involved with the police. Didn't want to file a missing person's report. I also got the feeling that the Andreyovs had rehearsed the answers they were giving me. Like they were playing some kind of a role. Also, Aleksi Kaledin's name came up, with Paul saying how helpful Kaledin had been to them."

"Helpful? How?"

"He just said – 'the store' – but I couldn't get anything more out of him."

Dorothea asks, "Do you think Kaledin might be connected to Andreyov's murder?"

"What makes you say that?"

"Just my suspicious mind. I mean, if they were involved in something to do with Andreyovs' store – and even though Andreyov told you Kaledin had been helpful – well – maybe they had some sort of disagreement. And with Kaledin being – as we suspect – Russian Mafia – well, those folks often end their disagreements…violently."

I shrug.

"I guess it could be something like that. But I'm going to hold off on any speculation, until we hear what the police come up with. For all we know, it could just be a robbery gone bad."

I switch gears.

"Now, I've got some questions for you."

"Like…?"

"First, how did you spot me going into Futura?"

"Because I was staking out the store."

"So late at night? Two hours after closing time?"

Dorothea shakes her head.

"Actually, no stakeout was called for, at that time of night. Not on the schedule. But I didn't have anything better to do, so I thought I'd see if there was any after-hours activity. I was about to leave, when I saw you in your Ninja outfit."

"Next question. Why didn't you report me?"

"Truthfully? I was about to call it in, when that tempting thought we've already discussed came to me."

I put her thought into my own words.

"That maybe I'd find something that could help you in your investigation of Kaledin? And that you could squeeze me for that information, in exchange for not turning me in? Do I have it right?"

"I plead guilty."

I can't help teasing her.

"Hey, Dorothea – not reporting a crime? Bending the law? Hell – breaking the law like that? That's sure not in the finest tradition of the FBI training manual."

She sighs. She bends her head forward, and I sense there is something seriously wrong here.

Dorothea finally answers me.

"No, Will, it's not in any training manual. In fact, this whole operation is not exactly in the finest tradition of anything!" she says, the bitterness clear in her voice. "In case you haven't noticed, I'm kind of out in left field on this investigation. No partner. No access to enough cars to carry out a successful tail. Just keep me out of it, until I learn my lesson."

"Learn your lesson? What does that mean?"

Dorothea clenches her hands into fists. And when she continues, her voice takes on a hard edge.

"He won't beat me down! He was also involved in the affair – just as much as I was!"

I review what Dorothea just said, and I'm pretty sure I know what's going on. Not something I want to get into. But I'm liking this Dorothea Marquez. And it's obvious she's hurting. So maybe I can help?

I ask, "I'm guessing the problem here is a soured relationship with someone in your office?"

"The classic story," she answers. "Never get involved with someone where you work – right? But I did. And, with one of the senior guys. Dumb, huh? Then, when I finally broke it off – oh, did I forget to mention that he's married? This is how he's paying me back. With Siberia-style assignments – like this surveillance of Kaledin."

"But you're hoping to turn this assignment to your advantage by coming up with some solid stuff on Kaledin, right?"

Dorothea nods.

"Yes. I was hoping..."

I think...and then I decide. Dorothea's made a stupid personal mistake. But she's a nice kid. So I'm going to help her, if I can.

I tell her, "Yeah, you weren't too bright...getting involved with him. But the whole deal was as much his doing as it was yours. And you don't deserve to suffer because he has rank on you. That's too one-sided. We have to change that. So, okay…I'll keep telling you what I find out, and maybe it'll help you."

Dorothea smiles and takes a deep breath.

"Will, you are something. Thank you very much. And from my end, if I can help you in any way, I will. Agreed?"

"Agreed," I confirm.

My phone rings. I check the time. It's close to 1:00 A.M. I'm going to let this one go to the answering service.

But of course, like always, I can't resist. So I pick up the receiver.

Guess who?

Boris, of course. Who else is going to call me at one o'clock in the morning?

"You hear the news?" he demands, with no preliminaries…no hellos.

I ask, "You mean about Paul Andreyov?"

"Of course!" he shoots back, making it sound like I'd have to be stupid to think it's anything else. Why do I put up with this?

"'What you going to do about it?" Boris demands.

"What am I supposed to do about it, Boris? I'm not the police."

Boris plows on.

"Natalia call me earlier. She say, Paul was going to see Kaledin, the bastard. With a message Nina wanted Paul to give to Kaledin."

"Wait a minute! Did you just say, Paul talked to Nina? Where is she?"

"Natalia say Nina wouldn't tell Paul where she is. All Nina wants is, to make sure that Paul gives Kaledin the message from her."

"What did the message say, Boris?"

"I don't know. And Natalia don't know. I ask her. She say, Paul did not tell her what it said. And then he left, to deliver the message to Kaledin, that bastard!"

"Boris, how did you get into the middle of this?"

"Because after Paul leaves, to go see Kaledin, Natalia calls me. She worries about Paul giving Nina's message to Kaledin.

"So I run and look for Paul. But I can't find him. And then I hear the news. And you know what? I think Kaledin killed Paul. No, I don't know why he did it. You are Mr. Detective, not me. You got to find out. Because I am now very much worried for Nina. You got to talk to Natalia!"

"All right, Boris. I will talk to Natalia. Although I'm sure the police are talking to her, and are learning everything there is to know. But I will talk to her."

"Good. And quick, too. I worry about Nina!"

I draw the line. "Boris, I'm tired, and I'm going home. I will talk to Natalia tomorrow!" And I hang up.

CHAPTER EIGHTEEN

When I arrive home a short while later, Lu is not in the hallway, as she usually is, with a welcome home kiss and my club soda on the rocks.

Instead, she is in our bed.

Now, under some circumstances this could lead to something more interesting than club soda.

But it *is* 2:00 a.m. so it's strictly talk time.

"What's happening, My Love?" Lu asks, as she wakes up when I come into the bedroom. She's a light sleeper, and no matter how hard I try to be quiet, Lu always wakes up when I come home late.

"Nothing interesting," I say.

And then I can't resist, and I tell her. "I just spent part of the night dressed up like a Ninja Warrior, and then a couple of hours with a beautiful young woman."

Nothing shakes up Lu. And besides, she knows me too well. So she comes back at me with…"I bet you looked good as a Ninja. Although from what I've read, most Ninjas are in their early or mid-20s. And as for the beautiful young woman, you sure she was with you, and not some other, younger Ninja?"

I sit down on the bed and give her a kiss.

"You know me too well," I tell her. "I just can't fool you."

"True. But all this talk about Ninjas and beautiful young women – I'm interested. Tell me all about it."

And I do.

And then I undress, brush my teeth and get into bed.

Next to Lu.

Nothing happens.

We go to sleep.

Sorry.

CHAPTER NINETEEN

"He said it had to be. Andreyov was getting too worried about Nina. Was talking about going to the police and filing a missing person's report."

The speaker is Anatole Guerin, and he is talking to Gregor Ramikin, in Russian, as they sit in Ramikin's office, in the latter's construction company in North Hollywood.

Ramikin, the older of the two men, is in his early fifties. He looks like the peasant stock from which he's descended. Short and broad, he has a round face, its most distinguishing feature being two pale gray eyes that bore coldly into whomever Ramikin is looking at.

Guerin, in his mid-thirties, is taller, about six feet, with a sculpted body developed in daily workouts in the weight room. He wears his long blond hair in a small pony tail, and his manner is crude and direct. Guerin is the sort who would rather go through a wall than bother to find a way around it.

Both Ramikin and Guerin are known to Ray Malik, the LAPD Russian Mafia expert – Ramikin as one of the upper echelon people in the organization, and Guerin as his main enforcer.

"I don't like it," Ramikin says. "Killing should only be when it is necessary. And I am not sure it was necessary with Andreyov."

"Fuckin' Kaledin goes off the wrong way, sometimes," Guerin says. He looks at his boss. "Some day, you're gonna want me to take care of him."

Ramikin smiles.

"Anatole, you must learn to see there is more than one side to things. Aleksi Kaledin has his shortcomings. That is true. But he also is very, very smart. So we have to concentrate on his good side. You see?"

Guerin nods.

"It's so, if you say so."

"And I do say so," Ramikin answers, effectively ending this part of their conversation.

Ramikin asks Guerin, "What about the girl? Aleksi hasn't been able to find her, has he?"

"No, but he tells me that there is now a private detective also looking for her. Someone her grandfather hired."

"Shit," Ramikin laughs. "Don't worry about him. Most private detectives could not find someone even if they had their address."

"This one is supposed to be different. Kaledin says the man used to be one of the best homicide detectives in the Los Angeles Police Department until he retired."

"You know his name? And where we can find him?"

"Will Jonas," Guerin answers. "And yes, I know where his office is."

"Good. If we ever have to deal with him, we will."

Ramikin smiles.

"So Aleksi and his men are looking for the girl. And now, this detective is looking also. Well, here is what you have to do, Anatole.

"If Aleksi finds her, just let him deal with the situation.

"But if this private detective finds the girl, then kill him. And bring the girl here, and we will deal with her."

CHAPTER TWENTY

When I get to my office the next morning, there's Boris, waiting for me. And I could swear he and Rose were holding hands before I arrived.

"You hang up on me last night," Boris booms. "What? You only work daytime?"

I tell him, "I did enough work for you yesterday. I don't have to keep going into the middle of the night."

"All right. All right. You the detective. You do it the way you have to. Just remember, my poor Nina is in danger."

Boris isn't Jewish. And he's not a woman. But, can he dump Jewish Mother Guilt? Must have been taking lessons from Rose.

"Okay," I tell Boris. "I'll go see Natalia as soon as I get through some phone calls I need to make. And you can come with me. In fact, why don't you call Natalia and set it up."

That satisfies him for the moment.

I go into my office and call Charlie Black, on the off-chance that he's on the Andreyov homicide.

"Yes," Charlie answers my question. It is his case.

"Why are you interested?" he asks. "You got something for me? Something I should know?"

"Maybe."

"Explain."

"You should talk to the owner of Futura Furniture – Aleksi Kaledin. Futura is down the block from Andreyov's store."

"Got the name and a rundown, already, from Ray Malik. Did so, as soon as I saw it was a Russian victim. I know Malik's been keeping tabs on Kaledin as a possible Russian Mafia guy. But why do *you* think Kaledin might be connected to the Andreyov killing? On the surface, it looks like a simple robbery and killing."

"Just a hunch, Charlie. Backed up by the following."

I fill Charlie in on my meeting with Kaledin. How Natalia and Paul Andreyov both seemed uptight at my mentioning Kaledin. How Natalia called Boris and told him Paul was going to see Kaledin, and could Boris try to stop him from doing so.

"Maybe it's all nothing," I tell Charlie, "but I got a feeling…"

"And you were pretty good with those feelings, when you were on the Job," Charlie muses. "I'll check it out. Got anything else?"

"Nothing right now," I tell him. "You'll let me know if you learn anything that will help me find this Nina?"

"Sure. And you're gonna do the same for me, right?"

"Would I do anything less for my old partner?"

"I sure hope not," Charlie says, hanging up.

As soon as I'm off the line, Rose buzzes me.

"Boris spoke to Natalia Andreyov. She didn't want to meet with you. But Boris – he insisted. He convinced her that she had to."

Now, I know Rose doesn't have access to a Congressional Medal of Honor, but if she did, I think she'd pin it on Boris. Yup. There's definitely some admiration going on between those two.

CHAPTER TWENTY-ONE

For someone whose husband was shot to death less than 24 hours earlier, Natalia Andreyov understandably is grieving.

But one look at her, as she opens the door to her small house in North Hollywood, and I suspect another, even stronger emotion, is gripping her.

Fear. Natalia Andreyov is scared.

"I do not know why you are here," she says defensively, holding the door only partially open, blocking our entry.

Boris isn't having any of it.

"Natalia, we got to talk," he says, putting his meaty paw on the door and pushing it inward until Natalia lets us in.

She says nothing, turns, and we follow her into a small living room. Natalia stops in the middle of the room and looks at us, her hands held tightly together, her arms across her breasts.

"Natalia," I say softly, trying to put her at ease, "you called Boris and asked him to intercept Paul and stop him from meeting with Aleksi Kaledin. Why?"

Natalia stiffens and hesitates before answering.

"I…I did not want Paul to bother Aleksi."

"What do you mean by…'bother'?"

"I just mean…Paul should not bother him. That's all."

Not going to get anywhere on that one, I decide, so I push in another direction.

"Natalia, we know that Nina called Paul and asked him to give Aleksi a message. What was that message?"

Natalia shakes her head.

"I do not know."

"Paul didn't tell you what Nina wanted him to tell Aleksi?"

"No. I ask him. He would not say. And…and then he leaves, to go see Aleksi."

Boris jumps in with the next question.

"Where was Nina calling from, Natalia? Where is my granddaughter?"

"Nina wouldn't tell Paul. He asked her. But she wouldn't tell him."

I ask Natalia, "The last time I was here, Paul said that Aleksi is good to you. In connection with the store. What does 'good' mean? What is Aleksi doing for you, with the store?"

Natalia shakes her head.

"I…I don't know what Paul means. He takes care of the store. Not me."

Boris cuts in.

"Natalia, you got to go to the police. You got to report that Nina is missing!"

Natalia shakes her head.

"You cannot tell me what to do. You will see. Natalia is coming back."

"You don't know that!" Boris roars.

Natalia flinches. Then she responds, her voice faint, but determined.

"Please go! I want you to leave now. Go!"

Boris is ready to do battle. But I can see that we're not going to get anything more from Natalia. She clearly is afraid of Aleksi. But getting her to tell us why – well, that will have to wait for another day.

I grab Boris and push him out of the house, me right behind.

Outside, Boris is agitated as hell.

"We got to go to Kaledin," he shouts at me. "The bastard knows something about Nina."

"He doesn't know where she is," I tell him. "I've already been over that with him."

"He lied to you," Boris answers. "We got to go!"

Actually, Boris isn't all that wrong. Another session with Kaledin might be useful. Maybe I could get out of him what, if any, success he was having in his search for Nina. And maybe, too, I could figure out some way to ask him about that sketch I found in his files.

"Hi, there, Aleksi. When I broke into your store, I found a really interesting sketch in one of the files in your office. Maybe you could tell me what it represents?"

Nah. That wasn't going to work. Give *that* tactic some more thought, please!

But there is one thing I don't have to give more thought to – I don't want Boris coming with me, to see Kaledin. As aggravated as Boris is, I don't want him anywhere near the guy.

He'll start ranting and raving, and Kaledin will clam up, for sure. No, it's better if I see Kaledin by myself.

I order Boris, "I want you to go back to my office and do some other things."

"What other things?"

He has me there. I have no idea what I meant when I said that to him. I just said it to keep him from coming with me to Kaledin.

But I'm a fast thinker.

I ask him, "You know the block where Futura Furniture is? I want you to put together a list of every store on that block that's owned by a Russian."

"Why you want me to do that?" Boris asks.

Actually, although I hadn't thought of it before, as soon as I tell Boris to put the list together, it makes sense to me, for this to be done.

That sketch I found in Kaledin's office has been bugging me. Why did Kaledin have it? What did it mean? Why did some of the stores have check marks next to them and others didn't? Once Boris puts the list together, maybe something will hit me.

"I don't know…" Boris starts to protest.

"Do it," I order. "Like you said, I'm the master detective!"

Yes, I do play back to Boris his own words to me, when we first met, but don't knock my style, because it works. Boris leaves me, hopefully on his way back to my office.

I take out my cell phone and call Rose.

"Rose," I say when she answers, "I'm sending Boris back to you, to do a list. He'll explain. And whatever you do, keep him busy. Occupied. I don't want him going anywhere he shouldn't. Like confronting Aleksi. You understand?"

"Nu. I can do that," she tells me. "In fact, I'm keeping him with me this evening. Melanie is cooking dinner for us."

So! Rose is taking Boris home? Hey, they may be old, but they sure are moving right along. More power to the two of them.

CHAPTER TWENTY-TWO

For support, Nina leans against the sink in the shabby ladies' room of the diner where she's now working. She turns on the cold water and splashes her face, then looks in the scratched mirror above the sink.

Staring back at her is a stranger – face strained, eyes blinking nervously, someone she almost doesn't recognize...doesn't know.

But of course she does know. It's herself. Frightened. Very frightened.

She tries to calm her nerves, as her mind plays back what is scaring her – the story she has just read in the San Francisco Chronicle.

Someone left the paper on the counter after lunch, and Nina saw the story when she picked up the paper, as she was clearing the dirty dishes. It was in the "California Report" column, a daily summary of news from around the state.

The first item in the column was headlined, "Russian Merchant Killed." It reported Paul Andreyov's killing, and provided a brief summary of what the police believed had happened – that the victim had surprised someone robbing his store, and the robber shot him.

But Nina knows better. She knows that Aleksi is replying to the message she had asked Paul to give him. Aleksi is telling her – don't send me messages through your relatives. I will kill them, one by one, unless you come back with that file.

Nina shakes her head.

Her original plan isn't working. She had hoped that if she stayed away, if she claimed she had a file from his computer, this would convince Aleksi that she wouldn't do anything as long as he left her family alone. It would be what some of her American friends call "a Mexican standoff."

But the plan isn't working.

She is certain that Aleksi killed Paul.

Who would be next?

Nina gasps.

It would be her grandfather! She is sure of it. Aleksi knows how much she loves Boris. Wonderful Boris. Not only her grandfather, but her best friend.

She could not let anything happen to him!

But what could she do? To keep Boris safe?

Should she return to Aleksi? Would that satisfy him?

No, that wouldn't end it. Not with Aleksi. Especially since she didn't really have any file! Just what she remembered seeing on his computer that day, before he came back.

She realized, now, how wrong she had been in her initial planning. All she had succeeded in doing was to anger Aleksi.

Anger him to the point where she was sure he intended to kill her. And Boris, too.

That is Aleksi!

So? What can she do, she asks her mirror reflection? What should she do now?

She nodded.

Yes. She knows the answer. Knows what she must do. To protect her beloved Boris. And herself.

She'll go back to Aleksi.

But only for one reason. To kill him!

Somewhere…somehow…she will find a gun. And she will kill Aleksi!

CHAPTER TWENTY-THREE

The next day, when I get to my office, Rose is there – but I don't see Boris.

And then, when I realize he's not in the office, I'm surprised at my reaction. I miss that crazy Russian. He takes up a lot of space when he's around – makes things more interesting.

"So, where's Boris?" I tease Rose. "I told you yesterday to make sure he stays in the office."

"And I did. And he did," she answers. "I even shlepped him home with me. He had dinner with us – with Melanie and me. And you know what? They got along very nicely. I can see what a wonderful grandfather he must be to that Nina."

"It looks to me like you and Boris are getting along very nicely, too."

Rose smiles. "It's been a *longa tseit* – a long time, Will – since a man gave me the kind of attention Boris does." She smiles again. "We will see."

The phone rings – Rose answers it, listens, then tells me, "FBI Special Agent Dorothea Marquez."

I go into my office and pick up.

"Dorothea…don't worry. I didn't do any Ninja breaking and entering last night."

"Good. I can only bend the rules so much."

"Well, no bending needed. So, what can I do for you?"

"It's what I may be able to do for you, for the next few weeks. That's why I'm calling."

"You have my attention. What do you mean?"

"My surveillance assignment on Futura Furniture and Aleksi Kaledin has been terminated, effective today. I'll be desk-bound – pretty much in the office – for the next couple of weeks. And…uh…because of what I told you…about that …relationship…things are going to be a little sticky. It'll get better…but not right away."

"But it *will* get better, right?"

"Yes. But I've decided, rather than suffer that awkwardness in the office – I'll take some vacation time. Been over a year since my last one."

"Good idea. What are you planning to do?"

"That depends on you, Will."

"On me? You have to explain that one."

"Well, I don't feel like going to some resort – alone. Or getting involved in something casual, while I'm there. So… I'm wondering if you could use some extra help, on the Nina search?"

"Not right now. But I have a feeling that's going to change. If so, how do I reach you? Not at the FBI office, right?"

"Right."

Dorothea gives me her portable and home phone numbers – and then, as we're ending our call, Rose runs into my office.

"Will! I just got a call from Valley Hospital. Boris is in the Emergency Room!"

"What happened?"

"I don't know. But that meshugana! That crazy man. I bet he went to see Aleksi Kaledin. I warned him not to. But I bet he went!"

CHAPTER TWENTY-FOUR

On the way to the hospital, my feelings keep ping-ponging. From fear to anger. From anger to fear.

Fear for how badly Boris may be hurt.

Anger directed at Aleksi Kaledin, if he put Boris in the hospital.

When we get there, we go to the Emergency Room reception desk and ask for Boris. The nurse asks if we are family – and before I say anything, Rose answers.

"The patient and I – we are engaged." She nodded toward me. "And he is Boris's cousin."

The nurse looks at us, not believing.

Rose puts a handkerchief to her eyes.

"Please," she pleads in a soft voice. "Please let us see him…"

Can *I* ever resist Rose in the office? No.

Can the *nurse* resist Rose here?

She buzzes us into the Emergency ward.

As we are going in, I ask Rose, "You and Boris are engaged? Since when?"

Rose smiles at me.

"Since never. But thank God it got us in, didn't it?"

Boris is in one of the cubicles, and as we near it, a doctor is leaving.

"Doctor," Rose says softly, "how is my husband?"

"Your husband will be fine," he answers Rose. "Heavy bruising on both sides of his rib cage, but nothing broken. We'll let him rest here for a few hours, and then you can take him home."

When the doctor leaves, I nudge Rose. "You get engaged at the reception desk, and married in the Emergency Room. Don't you think that's rushing things a little?"

Rose shrugs, and gives me her universal-for-everything answer. "Nu?"

We go into the cubicle to see Boris.

"How are you feeling?" Rose asks, her concern evident.

"I am all right. A little sore. But all right," Boris answers.

For the moment, they only have eyes for each other, but I'm not so happy about things.

"You went to Kaledin, right?" I demand.

Boris nods.

"What the hell were you thinking? I told you to stay away from him!"

"Don't yell. I'm not feeling so good," Boris whines.

He just gets better and better at guilt dumping, doesn't he? Must be getting lessons from Rose.

I look Boris over. He's sitting up in the bed. Seems a little weak, but otherwise okay.

"You're not so sick," I challenge him. "And goddamn lucky on that score. Why the hell did you go see Kaledin?"

"Because I had to!" Boris answers. "Nina is my granddaughter. I have to help her. I have to find out whatever Kaledin, that bastard, knows that could help me find Nina."

"And what did you find out?"

"Nothing," he admits.

But then he fixes me with that one-hundred-per-cent-I-am-right stare of his.

"But he knows something. I am sure of this!"

"And what might that something be?" I challenge him.

"I...do not know," Boris admits. "But he knows something," he adds lamely.

"How'd you get hurt?" I ask him.

"Kaledin's goon did it."

Kaledin's "goon?" Did he really use that word, from one of the old TV cop shows? Maybe *The Naked City*?

"Why'd Kaledin's guy do that?" I ask.

Boris hesitates, and then he says, "Because..."

Not good enough, Boris.

"That's not an answer. I want to know *why* he roughed you up."

Boris shrugs.

"Because I tried to hit Kaledin."

Boris looks defiantly at me.

"And you know what? I could beat him good, if his goon don't sneak up on me."

Boris The Battler. That's what I have here. A 70+ road warrior.

I've had enough of Boris for right now. And besides, I have things to do.

I tell Boris, "When they let you out of here, no more return visits to Kaledin. Understand?"

"I'll make sure," Rose promises.

"Good."

Boris isn't through, though.

"Where you going?" he asks.

"To Kaledin," I tell him.

"You hit him good for me," Boris orders.

CHAPTER TWENTY-FIVE

As much as I would have liked to do what Boris ordered, my goal in seeing Kaledin was not to hit him, but to get whatever information I could.

Like what message did the now-deceased Paul Andreyov deliver to him from Nina? That was the biggie, I was hoping, that could unravel the mystery of where Nina was hiding. And why?

Was Kaledin going to give me that information?

Very unlikely, but I had to try.

When I reach Futura Furniture, I wonder if I should carry my gun, but I decide against it. This isn't going to be that kind of a meeting, I was sure. Just he and I telling each other lies, hoping to learn something useful in the process.

I go into the store and head directly back, toward Aleksi's office. As I near it, a very large guy steps in front of me. I'm six four and I weigh 210. He's a couple of inches taller, and much, much broader from his neck down.

"Can I help you?" he asks.

Well, give the guy credit. He speaks nicely. Much better sounding than what I thought would come out of the mouth of an obvious bodyguard.

I can play nice-sounding, too.

"I'd like to see Mr. Kaledin, please. My name's Will Jonas. And this is about Nina. I'm sure he'll want to see me."

"Wait here, please."

The guy turns and goes into Kaledin's office. A minute later, he opens the door and smiles me in.

Once I'm in, I notice that the guy closes the door, and takes up a position directly in front of it. In other words, he's blocking my way out. Interesting.

I turn toward the front of the office, as Kaledin steps around from behind his desk. All business. And if he is surprised by my visit, he isn't showing it.

"Mr. Jonas? You said this is about Nina? May I ask your association with her, please?"

I figure this is no time to be subtle. Don't think that would gain me anything. So I go right at him.

"I'm a private investigator. I've been hired by Nina's grandfather – Boris – to find her. He says she's been missing for several weeks. That would make it...just about the time she left you."

For just an instant, Kaledin seems shaken. But he recovers quickly. He smiles and walks toward me, his hand extended to shake mine.

"What you say is very interesting. Please. Let's sit down and discuss it."

He nods to a sitting area – two easy chairs and a couch. We walk to it and sit down in the two chairs, facing each other.

"Yes," Kaledin says, "Nina and I were together for some time. Her grandfather is correct about that. But I have no idea where she went, when she left me. I've not been concerned, though. She's a very resourceful person. I'm sure she is off somewhere, doing whatever it is she wants to do."

"Her grandfather doesn't see it that way. He is very concerned with what might have happened to Nina since she left you. He's not heard from her since then."

"And you've been hired to find her?"

"That's right. I've been hired by Boris – who came to see you – and got a going over by one of your goons. Was it the guy back there, by the door?"

"Will – may I call you Will – you've got to understand that Igor is very protective of me. Boris came in here, threatening I don't know what – then attacked me, and Igor just stepped in and restrained him. I'm sorry if Boris was injured in that process. But he *did* come after me."

I decide to tone things back a little now – in the hope that I might learn something useful.

"Okay, I can understand that," I tell Kaledin. "But aside from that, maybe you can answer a few questions I have?"

Kaledin also seems ready to slow things down – I guess for the same reason – to see what he might learn from me. He nods, but before I can get started, another oversized guy comes into the office and takes a position next to the bodyguard already at the door. Kaledin gives him a quick head shake and this second guy turns and leaves.

Kaledin picks up the conversation.

"So, tell me, Will – may I call you Will – do you have any…encouraging information about where Nina might be?"

"Actually," I counter, "I think you might have more and better information than I have."

"Oh? I don't understand what you mean."

"What I mean is – I know Paul Andreyov came to see you last night. After he talked to Nina, and she gave him a message for him to give to you."

Aleksi shakes his head.

"I never saw Paul last night. And this morning, I heard on the news that he was killed in his own store. And the police say it was some robber? Is that right? A terrible thing. No one is safe anymore."

I decide I'm not going to learn anything from continuing the discussion with Aleksi.

But I also decide to give Igor a lesson.

I stand and walk up to him, by the office door. I stop and stare at him.

He tries to stare me down, but I'm almost as tall as he is, so that doesn't work for him.

I move in closer, staring, keeping my eyes locked on his. Deliberately, I keep my hands down, non-threatening, at my sides, so that his attention stays on our staring contest.

Now, I come closer to him – just a couple of inches separating us.

I keep staring, and so does he.

Eyes to eyes.

So he never sees me bring my knee up – hard – right into his balls.

Igor doubles over, grabbing for his crotch with both hands. Good again.

I lock my hands together and bring them down on top of the guy's head, while at the same time jerking my knee up again. And since he is doubled over, my knee catches him right on the jaw.

Igor collapses on the floor. No more problem with him.

I turn to Aleksi, who is staring at me but not daring to move.

"That's for Boris," I tell him. "Don't ever let this ape touch Boris again, or it'll be your balls the next time."

Well, so much for my trying to learn anything from Kaledin. Ah, what the hell – aside from Nina, we didn't seem to have anything in common, and he wasn't giving me any useful information, anyway.

I look down at the guy on the floor. He's still on his side, his back toward me, still groping where it hurts. I give him a hard boot in the ass.

"You get anywhere near Boris, and you and I are going to meet again," I warn him. "And I won't be so nice next time."

I walk out of the office, through the store, and out the front door.

Move over, John Wayne!

CHAPTER TWENTY-SIX

Gregor Ramikin laughs.

"You mean that Jonas was so tough?" he asks Anatole Guerin, "that he hit Igor in the balls, knocked him down and then kicked him?"

"I was there, at Futura, when this Jonas did it to Igor," Guerin said. "He did it very well. Even if he is an old man."

Ramikin looks at Guerin, a teasing smile on his face.

"Maybe old in years, but he knows how to fight. To win. So, maybe he could do to you, what he did to Igor? Maybe that Jonas could knock you in the balls, too?"

Guerin bristles at the teasing.

"He would not have a chance with me," he says, then adding pragmatically, "especially now that I know how he fights. I would be ready for him."

Ramikin pats Guerin on the shoulder, an affectionate pat.

"I believe you, my friend."

Then Ramikin changes subjects.

"Aleksi was really stupid enough to have that old man, Boris, beaten up?"

"It would have been worse, if I didn't stop Igor. Aleksi was doing nothing to stop it. I think Igor would have killed the old man."

Ramikin shakes his head.

"It would have been a senseless killing, an unnecessary killing, and not a good thing. It would draw too much attention, and that would not be good for our plans with Aleksi."

Guerin says, "Some day you will tell me to kill him."

"Perhaps, perhaps. But for right now, he is too valuable to me."

Ramikin thinks for a moment before he speaks again.

"The detective, this Will Jonas, you will stay close to him," he orders Guerin. "The more I learn about him, the more capable he appears to be. If anyone can find the girl, it probably will be this man."

CHAPTER TWENTY-SEVEN

Let's face it, I tell myself, on the way back to my office, I need to go to San Francisco to look for Nina. Boris has a strong feeling that's where she's hiding. And it makes sense to me, too. Fourth largest city in California. Good place for her to get lost.

I like San Francisco, but I wasn't looking forward to the trip. Finding someone who didn't want to be found, in a city of more than 725,000 people, wasn't going to be easy, especially for a one-man show like me. No police department backup, either.

And I was worried about something else, too. The safety of Rose and Boris…and Lu. There already was one death connected to this Nina search – Paul Andreyov. And I'd no doubt pissed off Aleksi Kaledin when I visited him. Put all that together, and I was not comfortable leaving those three, while I was in San Francisco.

My solution? I decide to take Dorothea Marquez up on her offer. When I get back to my office, I dial her home number.

When she picks up, I tell Dorothea, "Okay, you still want to help me out?"

"Absolutely," Dorothea answers. "What can I do?"

"I need to go to San Francisco. And I'm worried about the safety of Rose and Boris – and my wife, Lu. Can you spend the next few days watching out for everyone? I'd really appreciate it."

"When do you want me to start?"

"If you can, please come over to the office today, so I can introduce you to Rose and Boris, and bring you up to date on what's happening with Aleksi Kaledin. Then, I'd like you to come home with me to meet Lu. And if you can stay for dinner, that would be great."

"Gee, a bodyguard with dining privileges," Dorothea says. "What a deal."

CHAPTER TWENTY-EIGHT

As agreed, Dorothea came to dinner with Lu and me.

The two of them hit it off well, although Lu really didn't think the need was there for protection.

"Will," she pointed out, "you've told me before that Mafia types don't usually attack the families of their adversaries. Families are kept out of it."

"Used to be true," I allowed, "but that pattern is changing."

"Especially with the Russian and other Eastern European Mafia," Dorothea added. "We've definitely seen this at the Bureau. These people will kill everybody and anybody. And with no hesitation."

"Okay, so how do you carry out this…protection?" Lu asked. "Are you going to be with me all of the time? That's not possible, is it? Especially since you're also going to be watching out for Rose and Melanie, and this Boris person."

"Dorothea will rotate among you. Sometimes watching you. Other times, Rose. And I'm asking Rose to keep Boris and Melanie close to her."

"When does all this start?" Lu asked.

"Once I fly up to San Francisco," I told her. "And most of the time, you won't even be aware that Dorothea is covering you."

CHAPTER TWETY-NINE

The next day, I take a late morning Southwest flight out of Burbank, rent a car at the San Francisco Airport and get to the city around two o'clock.

I check into a motel on Lombard Street. Clean, modern, doesn't cost an arm and a leg. My kind of place.

In my room, I plan how I'm going to search for Nina.

Fact: I know from Boris that Nina doesn't have much money. She wasn't working while she was living with Aleksi. So here in San Francisco, she probably is staying in one of those rent-a-room-by-the-week places. Maybe out in North Beach. Good place for me to start.

Fact: Boris also told me that before she met Aleksi, Nina had done some waitressing. Not regularly, but enough for spending money.

Well, that might be something she'd do up here. Not a high-end restaurant, though. Aside from probably not having enough experience for that, she'd have to give the management her Social Security number and other personal data. She wouldn't want to do that, if she was trying to hide.

No, if she did any waitressing, it'd be in one of the more casual places that wasn't so uptight about its record keeping. Probably a cheap diner. Some place that might even pay her in cash, to save some payroll costs. Plenty of those I could check out.

Before I came to my room, I'd bought a copy of the *San Francisco Examiner*. And now, I went through the "Apartments For Rent" section.

There were plenty of rentals in North Beach and the surrounding areas. So it was clear what I had to do. I needed to walk the streets, show Nina's picture around and see what I could find.

CHAPTER THIRTY

And that's what I did, for the rest of the day, and for two more days, going street by street, talking to apartment house and restaurant managers.

Not my idea of a fun job, but it had to be done. And late in the afternoon on the second day, I hit pay dirt at one of the crummier apartment buildings, on Stockton.

"She looks different than that picture, but it's her," Clara Bowden, the manager, tells me when I show her Nina's photo.

Good news! Now, at least I can confirm that Nina had come to San Francisco when she left Los Angeles. Boris had been right about that.

"She here now?" I ask Clara.

She shakes her head.

"Left a week ago. Sudden-like, too. Still had two days on the week's rent that she paid."

"Do you know where she went? Did she leave any forwarding address?"

"No."

"Did she tell you if she was working? And if so, where?"

Clara thinks about it.

"We didn't talk much. She wasn't your real friendly type. But one day, I was coming in when she was going out, and she was dressed in what looked like a waitress outfit. Blouse and skirt. And the name of the place on the blouse. You know, on the pocket."

Clara pauses and looks at me. I know the look. It means, I know something you want to know. How much is it worth to you?

I take out the twenty-dollar bill that I had folded into my shirt pocket, anticipating this kind of a hold up.

The twenty passes from me to Clara with the speed of light.

"Danny's Diner," she tells me. "Over on Green Street."

A little while later, I walk into Danny's Diner. And yes, it's the kind of place I figure Nina would be working in.

And there *is* a Danny. And he does remember Nina. Although she told him her name was Sally Wertman. Sally Wertman? Where'd she get that one?

As it was with Clara, the trail at Danny's is a week cold. The same day Nina left Clara's apartment building, she hadn't shown up to work the lunch shift at Danny's, nor any time since then.

"And there was somebody here, waiting for her that day, too," Danny says.

Uh oh. My worry antenna goes up.

"Someone was here, waiting for her the day she didn't show up?" I confirm.

"That's right. Big guy. Had an accent. I think it was Russian. He talked the same way Sally talked. And when I'd asked her, she told me she was originally from Russia."

I think back to my meeting with Aleksi Kaledin, and his two muscle bound pals.

The one who'd greeted me at Aleksi's office door didn't have any accent. He was USA Beef all the way.

And the other guy? The one who came into Aleksi's office, but then was waved off by Kaledin? I don't know if he was Russian, or what, because he didn't say anything.

I ask Danny to describe the guy. No, I decide when he finishes, the man waiting for Nina at Danny's is not the same person who'd stepped into Kaledin's office when I was there.

So, who was he? Another of Kaledin's guys?

You can bet on it, I tell myself.

And this worries me. Because, whoever he is – he has at least a week's head start on me.

Of course, when I met with him, Kaledin didn't mention he had people up in San Francisco, looking for Nina. But why should he? I knew I was going up there, and I didn't tell Kaledin. So much for our cooperating in our search, right? No surprise there.

Chapter Thirty-Two

By now, it's getting close to six o'clock – a bad time to be trying to get the attention of restaurant and apartment building managers – so I decide to go back to my motel, write up my notes and plan out what places to cover tomorrow.

When I get back to my room, I can tell that someone's been through it.

Maybe the maid, doing her evening thing? You know – turn down the bedspread, leave the chocolate on the pillow?

Only this isn't a chocolate-on-the-pillow kind of place.

Just to make sure, I call the front desk. The desk clerk tells me that no maid would have had any reason to come into the room.

So how did I know that someone *had* been in my room?

Because of a sneaky habit that I have, whenever I'm working a case and I stay in a hotel.

Whenever I leave my room, I arrange some items on the desk into a special pile. Now, in the room where I'm staying, there are three different tourist magazines on the desk, plus a card asking for the occupant's opinion about the hotel's services, and seven flyers for restaurants in the area. I arrange these items on the desk top, and if they are not arranged the same way when I return, then I know someone has been in the room.

And voilá – as that French detective with the little moustache would say – the desk top arrangement is a little bit different than how I'd set it up.

Conclusion: someone definitely has been in the room.

I check out the rest of the room. Nothing is missing. Everything seems okay.

So, the questions are – who came into my room? And why? Is it one of Kaledin's people? Does Kaledin have someone following me?

I haven't spotted any tail. But then again, I haven't been looking for one. I don't know San Francisco all that well, so I've been checking my street map, as I've gone to the apartment houses and diners. Under those conditions, I'm not likely to see any tail.

My thoughts are interrupted by the telephone ringing.

It's Boris.

"Nina called me," he starts right in, no preliminaries. "She wants to see you. Right away."

CHAPTER THIRTY-ONE

Here's how Boris explains it to me.

"Nina just call me. She say she is in San Francisco. I say, you are there, too, looking for her.

"She ask, who are you? And why are you looking for her? I tell her, because I am worried and I hire you to find her.

"She say, she don't want to be found. Everyone is looking for her, but she don't want to be found. By no one.

"I ask her, why is that? What kind of trouble you in? Got to be trouble, to be acting like this.

"She starts crying, my Nina. I can't stand it! I want to be there. I want to hold her. Stop her crying.

"Anyway, I say to her she got to tell me what's going on. Why is she hiding? Why she leave Aleksi?

"She don't want to tell me, but I yell at her she got to tell me. So, finally she say she run away from Aleksi, because he is bad.

"So what? I say to her. I told you a long time ago he was no good, but that is no reason to hide. You come back to me, your grandfather. I take good care of you.

"She tell me she can't do that. She tell me that she is afraid for my life, if she comes back.

"I don't believe what I am hearing. What does all this mean?

"I yell at her again, so she finally tell me. She say that Aleksi, that bastard, he threatens to kill me.

"But why? I ask her.

"She tell me, because she – Nina—thinks she knows what Alexi is doing with the Russian Mafia. It is bad. And she know about it."

I manage to interrupt Boris the first time he stops to take a breath.

"You say she wants to see me. Where is she in San Francisco? And what's this about what the Russian Mafia and Kaledin are doing? And her knowing about it?"

"She don't say any more," Boris tells me. "Only that she will talk to you about everything, because she hopes you can help."

"So? Where is she?" I ask again.

"I write it down," Boris says.

There's a pause and I assume he's looking for what he wrote down. Then he's back on the line.

"She say, to meet her at ten o'clock tomorrow morning, at the corner of Folsom Street and Fourth Street."

I know enough about San Francisco to realize that's the address for the Moscone Convention Center.

Now, Boris gives me more directions.

"She say you should stand there, and she will come to you. I tell her what you look like. And you got her picture, right?"

"Right," I confirm.

"Jonas, you got to help her," Boris pleads. "You got to help her against that bastard Kaledin. You know, I want to go see him again. But Rose and your crazy FBI lady, they stop me."

I send a silent "thank you" to Rose and Dorothea, and I shout at Boris.

"You stay away from Kaledin! You understand? Stay away from him!"

"Okay. Okay," Boris answers.

I want more assurance.

"Is Dorothea there now?" I ask him.

"Sure," Boris says. "She and Rose. They don't leave me alone, almost not even when I got to pee."

Boris, Boris – you sure are a refined kind of guy.

I tell him, "Let me talk to Dorothea."

Dorothea comes on the line.

"Will? You okay?"

"Yeah. Listen, you have to keep Boris from going back to see Kaledin. It would be dangerous."

"Don't worry," Dorothea says. "I told Boris I'd shoot him in the kneecap if he tries to get out of my sight. I think he almost believes me."

"Good. Please keep it that way."

"Will, what's going on? What's all this talk about Kaledin and the Russian Mafia? Anything I should know, for my office?"

"Not clear yet. But I think I'll know a lot more, once I meet Nina tomorrow morning. I'll fill you in after that."

"Will?"

"Yes?"

"Be careful."

CHAPTER THIRTY-TWO

"Today, that private detective found the last places where the girl lived and worked," Gregor Ramikin *reports, when his contact answers his call.*

"And...?"

"Then he went back to his hotel. Anatole tells me he is still there. Probably for the night. But who knows?"

"Who knows? I want to know! I don't want questions! I want answers!"

"Yes. Yes. I understand," Ramikin *assures him.* *"I understand."*

"You make sure Anatole stays on him!" the contact orders, *before hanging up.*

CHAPTER THIRTY-THREE

So...now that I know someone is tailing me here in San Francisco, I need to figure out how to lose the tail, when I go to meet Nina tomorrow.

I figure there are at least two people involved. Earlier today, one of them likely followed me around North Beach, while the other searched my room.

Who are they?

Easy answer to that question. Have to be Kaledin's people.

He hadn't had any success yet in finding Nina. He knew I was looking for her, too. So he's hedging his bets. If his people can't find her, maybe I can.

So, how do I lose the tail – before I meet Nina tomorrow morning? Here's what I figure I need to do.

First, I have to make sure the tail believes one hundred per cent that I don't know I'm being followed.

And second, I have to make them feel that I am becoming very predictable in my actions. Give them a sense of security – that I will be doing tomorrow pretty much what I'm doing today.

So, even though I know that nighttime canvassing of diners and apartment houses won't result in much, I decide to keep going tonight, anyway. Let the tails see I'm doing the same thing I've been doing all along.

At eight o'clock, I drive my car out of the motel's parking area and take Lombard toward North Beach. After a few blocks, I check my mirror for the tail.

There it is. An Oldsmobile, making all the right moves as the driver follows me. Good. Stay with me, fella.

For the next couple of hours, I canvass some apartment houses and diners. No positive results, but that's okay. I'm doing this for the tail's benefit.

By ten o'clock, I'm back in my room.

I check the desk in the room. Everything is as I left it. No visitors this time.

I call an Open-24-Hours car rental agency. Not the agency I'm renting from now. Another one. I arrange to pick up a car early the next morning.

Then, I go down to the lobby and ask the desk clerk some questions. After getting my answers, I go back to my room, set my traveling alarm clock for 5:00 a.m. and go to sleep.

CHAPTER THIRTY-FOUR

The next morning, at 6:00 a.m., I take the elevator down to the garage. But instead of going to my car, I follow the directions the desk clerk gave me last night, and walk to the exit door that leads to an alley behind the motel.

I open the door and look out. The alley is empty. I leave the garage and walk to the left, away from Lombard, toward Chestnut.

When I reach the end of the alley, I look out on to Chestnut. No Oldsmobile, like the one tailing me last night.

Good.

The last two mornings, at about 10:00 a.m., before I realized I was being tailed, I'd routinely driven straight out of the motel garage. And then last night, when I knew about the tail, I also drove out the same way, on purpose. I'm hoping that the tail will be expecting me to do the same today – in about four or so hours.

I walk east on Chestnut for a few blocks until I see a cab, wave it over and give the driver directions to the car rental office, which is on Market, near Van Ness.

When I check out the new rental car, it's only seven in the morning, which means I have three hours to kill before meeting Nina. So I do the sensible thing.

I drive over to the Moscone Convention Center, park in the garage, and try to nap. Not that comfortable in the car, but "war is hell," someone once said, so I manage to put up with it.

The alarm I had set on my wristwatch wakes me at 9:30. I leave the car and walk to the Center lobby, where there are the first stirrings of the on-site convention – the International Society of Computer Programmers.

Walking across the lobby to the bank of glass doors, I look out toward the corner of Folsom and Fourth. It's now a quarter to ten. Fifteen minutes until I'm supposed to meet Nina.

Staying in the lobby, I keep checking the pedestrian traffic flow, looking for Nina. And also looking for any men who seem to be just hanging around.

No Nina.

None of Kaledin's guys.

I wait until a couple of minutes to ten. Then I exit the lobby and walk toward the corner of Folsom and Fourth. I get there at ten on the dot.

I wait. And wait.

Nina arrives at 10:10.

I'm looking up Folsom, when she comes up on my right side, along Fourth.

"You are Will Jonas?"

I examine her. Although she's heavy on the makeup, and her hair is a different color and style than what her picture shows, it definitely is Nina.

"Yes. I'm Will Jonas."

Nina is nervous. Her eyes move around, checking in all directions.

I take her by the elbow.

"Come on, let's get away from here. Let's go where we can talk."

Nina pulls away from me and turns toward the Moscone Center.

"No. First we must go in there," she says.

I don't ask her, why. Don't want to push her – yet.

We walk into the lobby.

Nina asks, "Can you please buy tickets for us to go inside the exhibition hall?"

Now I'm getting edgy. Going inside was not what I had in mind.

"Why?" I want to know.

"Because there is something in there I must show you. It is important!"

I decide I might as well go along. I figure whatever it is that Nina wants to show me – I'll learn more about her problem than I know now.

I buy the tickets and we go into the exhibition hall. I look around and see more displays of computers and computer-related products than I can, or want, to count.

"Okay," I say, taking Nina by the shoulders and turning her toward me, "What are we doing here? What's this all about?"

"I need to use a computer, to write something down, to show to you," she says, and she heads toward a display of computers which have been set up by one of the exhibitors, so that people can try them out.

She sits down, opens the computer and starts it up. I don't know what the hell she is doing, but she seems pretty comfortable doing it.

Then she starts writing some sort of a list.

After she does a few names, I recognize them as stores in the same area as Futura Furniture. There are names of people next to each of the stores. And some of the stores have percentage numbers next to them.

Nina looks up at me.

"I found this on Aleksi's computer. I think he is doing something with the stores. But what...I do not know.

"I was going to print out a copy of the full file, but he came back too soon. I...I thought that if I had the file, I could bargain with Aleksi. That I could go away from him. And then, that he would leave my grandfather and me alone. If I promised not to give the file to anyone. Not to the police. Not to anyone like that."

She fights back the tears.

"But I was wrong to think that way. When I asked Paul Andreyov to give Aleksi a message...Paul was killed. I am sure it was Aleksi who killed him. And then I knew...I knew that even if Aleksi thought I had the file, it would not stop him. He would kill my grandfather. And then me."

I look at what Nina had written. And then I think back to what I'd seen in Kaledin's office – that sketch of stores, with check marks.

And I wonder – could this be something that Dorothea and the FBI could use? Any "probable cause" material here, that would give them enough to ask for – and get – a search warrant for Futura Furniture and Kaledin's office and files?

It seems to me that there is enough.

Nina interrupts my thinking.

"There…there is only one way to stop Aleksi," she says to me. "He…he has to be killed. Before he kills my grandfather. I have to kill him. Will you help me?"

Nina looks at me. I can see that she is nearing the end of her string. She gives her lower lip a couple of chews before continuing.

"My grandfather says you want to help me. If this is true, then you must help me kill Aleksi Kaledin!"

CHAPTER THIRTY-FIVE

I should help her kill Aleksi Kaledin?

Whoah! Not today, Nina! Not any day at all!

Fact is, I have killed before. Once while I was still in uniform. The other time when I was first starting out in Homicide as a rookie detective. Both were ruled justifiable shootings by an LAPD internal review board.

But my name isn't Paladin, and this isn't that old *Have Gun, Will Travel* television series.

"You can't be serious," I tell Nina.

She grabs my arm.

"You don't understand! If you don't kill Aleksi, he will kill Boris."

"Hold on," I tell her. I see a refreshment room off to one side of the hall. "Let's have some coffee and talk about this."

So we do.

And I tell her, "Look, Nina…what you showed me on the computer, and what I saw in a file, when I broke into Kaledin's office – yeah, I did break in there a few night ago – makes me think that the two things together are enough to interest the FBI. I know they're looking at Kaledin, and they've had him under surveillance, but they are having a hard time finding anything. Well, the information you and I have may be enough for them to take on the investigation. And more important – to protect you and your grandfather."

"Can…can you be sure about this?"

"Not 100 per cent. But I've got a good contact with the FBI. And you and I will go right to that person, as soon as we can get back to Los Angeles. Okay?"

Nina looks at me, and I can see that she wants to believe me. I sense that when she asked me to kill Aleksi, it was an act of desperation, and if there is some other way, she'd prefer it.

But still, she has her doubts.

"You are not the police. Not the FBI. How can you make these promises?"

"Because I have the right connections. Remember, I was a police officer for thirty years. And right now, I'm working with an FBI agent. In fact, she's already protecting Boris, for me."

For the first time since we met, Nina smiles.

"You mean, the lady who won't let Boris go to the bathroom by himself? He told me about her."

"That's the one," I say, grateful that Dorothea made such a strong impression on Boris that he told Nina about her.

And so what if I'm no longer LAPD? I know Charlie will jump on this. And so will Ray Malik.

I stand up.

"Come on, Nina. We have to get back to Los Angeles."

I turn toward the door leading out of the refreshment room and into the exhibition hall, and then I see him.

It's quick. But I see him before he ducks behind an exhibit booth. It's the guy who came into Kaledin's office at Futura, but didn't stay when Kaledin motioned to him to leave.

CHAPTER THIRTY-SIX

Natalia Andreyov watches Aleksi Kaledin walk up the short path to the front door of her house. She knew he would be coming. Ever since she stopped answering the telephone last night. And especially today, when she had not gone to open the store. To do the processing.

It doesn't matter. Nothing matters.

She is tired. She doesn't care what happens to her. Hasn't cared since that first moment she learned that Paul was dead.

Natalia sighs. How little Paul and she had known when they came to the United States, to Los Angeles, and had been befriended by Aleksi.

It seemed so simple. So easy. True, it was not exactly right. The way they ran the store. She and Paul knew this from the beginning. But Aleksi said, "This is America. Capitalism. No one cares, as long as everyone makes money."

So they had gone along with Aleksi.

But now it was over.

She hears the front door open. She hadn't bothered locking it. What for?

"Natalia?"

Aleksi's call is calm, friendly, as always.

Natalia cannot remember ever hearing Aleksi speak angrily. It isn't his way. He does terrible things, she now knows, but he always speaks so nicely.

"Natalia," Aleksi says again as he comes into the living room, where she is seated on the couch, waiting.

She doesn't respond.

Aleksi walks to the couch and stands over her.

"I expected you to open the store this morning, Natalia. It is necessary. For the processing."

Natalia looks up at Aleksi.

"It was wrong," she says. "It was wrong from the beginning."

Aleksi smiles as he brings the gun with its silencer out of his coat pocket and points it at Natalia.

"Whatever is wrong can always be fixed," he says. "You should have remembered that, Natalia."

But Natalia no longer has the ability to remember, as Aleksi shoots her in the head.

CHAPTER THIRTY-SEVEN

Damn! How'd he find us here? I ask myself. So they *did* have a tail on me when I left the hotel. I just didn't see it!

"What is it? What is the matter?" Nina asks, seeing my concern.

"One of Kaledin's people is here! I just spotted him, out in the exhibition hall."

"Oh no!" she cries, doubling over and hugging herself.

I decide it's got to be Tough Love time now! I grab Nina's arm and pull her up.

"Listen, Nina. You have to be strong now! We have to get to Los Angeles. You'll be safe there, and all of this will be over. You understand? You have to be strong. For your grandfather and you!"

Nina straightens up some, and I can almost see her reaching down inside herself and trying to bounce back from her despair.

"You are right," she says.

"Okay, let's go!" I tell her.

We leave the refreshment room and go into the exhibition hall. By now, the hall is starting to fill up with convention attendees, and I'm hoping we can lose ourselves in the crowd. Or at least put some distance between us and Kaledin's guy.

Guys, I correct myself. There has to be more than one of them.

We start walking, pushing into the crowd that's beginning to fill up the aisles of the exhibition hall.

I keep checking behind us, ahead of us, on both sides – trying to spot not only the man I had just seen, but anyone else who is part of that crew.

No luck. But I'm not surprised. The crowds are heavy now. Easy for them to keep hidden.

As we walk, I keep thinking ahead, trying to figure out what's best for us.

Should we go for the front exit to the Convention Center? Try to get out to Folsom and then lose ourselves in the street traffic?

No. There probably will be someone covering that way out. Pick up our trail right away.

How about down to the garage? To my car?

They'll have that covered, too. Since they know we are here, this means they followed me from the motel, to the car rental agency, and then into the Center's garage. So that escape route is out.

Suddenly, a man comes out of a side aisle and makes a grab for Nina. At the same time, another man comes at me from the other side and pulls at me.

Nina screams as my hold on her arm is broken and the guy starts pulling her away from me.

The other man is pulling at my left arm with both his hands. This leaves my right arm free, Nina having been pulled from it. I swing hard with my right fist and land it solidly on the side of my attacker's head.

He crashes into a nearby display, taking a few people down with him. Lots of shouting and screaming from that action. Good! The more confusion, the better.

I look to my right. Nina is screaming, and at the same time – good girl – she's scratching at her attacker's face. He is controlling her – but barely.

I jump at the guy and hit him, palm up, with the heel of my hand, aiming for the bottom of his nose. Contact! I hear the crack as his nose breaks, and the blood starts pouring out as he falls backward, into a product display on that side of the aisle.

People are shouting and screaming. Lots of crowd confusion. All good for our side.

I grab Nina's hand and pull her down a nearby side aisle, toward a door that I see at the end of the aisle.

Although we've gotten away from those first two attackers, I'm certain there is at least one more person tracking us – the man I first spotted a couple of minutes ago. And there could be more people with him!

We reach the door, I open it, and we run into a hallway that curves up ahead, out of sight.

I make a guess that we are in one of the halls that service the various parts of the Center, the back room stuff, where the workers set up the exhibits.

We run down the hall, around the curve and into a larger room.

I'm right. There are several people in here, assembling displays.

I stop to get my bearings and hear the footsteps behind us. I turn and see them.

Three men. The big guy from Kaledin's office, and two new people I don't recognize. I guess the two I had hit are still out of commission. I sure hope so.

When the men see we are in with a room full of people, they slow up. But they don't stop. They keep coming.

We can't stay here. Even with the people all around, those guys will be able to take us.

I spot a double door at the other end of the room. It's the only way out, except for the hall we'd just come through.

"Come on," I grab Nina's hand, "through there!"

We run across the room. Some of the workers stop to look at us, others don't bother.

We reach the double door. The three men are still coming. Still walking, not wanting to attract any attention. But they're getting close. Maybe forty, fifty feet behind us.

I push open the double door, and Nina and I run out – and right back into the convention hall!

This is getting us nowhere. What to do? In a few seconds, those goons will be coming through the door.

I decide.

And it's not my most responsible moment. I'm not proud of what I am about to do. In fact it's against the law. But it's our only chance.

Pulling Nina with me, we run out a few yards into one of the main aisles in the convention hall.

And then I start shouting.

"Fire! Fire! Fire!"

Of course, everyone in the immediate area pays attention. And that's just what I want.

I point in the direction of the double door through which Nina and I have just come.

"Out that way!" I shout. "Everyone out that way! Fire! Everyone out that way."

And it works!

Especially as I continue to shout "fire" and keep shoving people toward the double door.

In just a few seconds, the aisle fills up with people running through the now open double door. I look for the three goons and don't see them. I'm hoping that they've been kept from going forward by the heavy flow of people running in the opposite direction.

This gives Nina and me the break we need. We run toward a door that has an exit sign over it.

This isn't the front entrance, but one of the many doors, I suspect, that open from the inside but are locked on the outside. Doors that usually are used by the exhibitors to bring their wares into the Center. And unless Kaledin has an army of men out there, it's unlikely that he'll be covering these doors in the same way as the main entrances and exits. I sure hope so.

We luck out. The door is exactly what I suspected it would be. A direct exit to Third Street.

I look out. As near as I can tell, there's no one out there, watching for us.

Of course, right now, I'm not so sure about my ability to spot any tail or lookout. I'd sure screwed up earlier today.

Okay, get past that. And let's get moving.

Nina and I start running down Third toward Market Street.

"Where are we going?" Nina asks.

"To the BART station," I tell her.

CHAPTER THIRTY-EIGHT

When I told Nina we were going to the BART station, the only thing I had in mind was to get away from the Moscone Center as fast as we could.

The nearest BART station was at Powell and Market. When we get there, a train is ready to leave and we get on it. The next stop will be the Civic Center, and as we ride toward it, a plan starts taking shape in my mind.

When we arrive at the Civic Center station, I check around us. Don't see anyone, and I'm hopeful that we're not being followed.

"What do we do now?" Nina asks.

"We go to Los Angeles," I tell her.

"How do we get to the airport?"

"We don't. We're going to drive to Los Angeles. I'm sure that Kaledin's people will be covering the San Francisco Airport. Probably the San Jose and Oakland ones, too."

I start laughing.

"Why are you laughing?" Nina asks, puzzled. I think she's also alarmed that I *can* laugh, given our present situation. Wondering what kind of a nut I might be.

"I'm laughing because I have to rent another car. This will be the third one I've rented in the last 72 hours. And I haven't returned the first two, yet. Come on. Let's find a telephone booth."

We locate a booth. I call a car rental company that has an office on Market, close to where we are now. I arrange for us to pick up a car in 15 minutes.

I'm tempted to call the other two car rental companies and ask them to do their own pickups, but I decide to leave those cars where they are. Chances are Kaledin will have men watching both, and the longer they stay in place, the more he might believe we're still in San Francisco. An expensive decoy game, but one I figure I should play.

The same with my motel. Unless I call and tell them I'm checking out, I'll be charged this upcoming night for a room I won't be using.

Can't be helped, though. I don't want to take the chance that Kaledin might learn I'd left, so I'm going to let the reservation stand. Tomorrow, I'll cancel the room and tell the car rental agencies where their vehicles are.

Okay, with all the housekeeping stuff now taken care of, I need to call Los Angeles.

Because Dorothea and I had worked out the plan before I left for San Francisco, I know that she, Rose, and Boris are at Boris's house in Canoga Park.

I call Boris's number. Rose answers, and I tell her to put the call on the phone's loudspeaker, "So everyone can hear."

Rose does, and Boris barges right in.

"You got Nina? You got my granddaughter with you?"

Well, I can't blame him.

"Yes, I've got Nina. Here. Talk to her."

I hand the phone to Nina.

"Dedushka! Dedushka!" Nina shouts the Russian word for grandfather. "I'm here. I love you."

"You are all right, my Nina? You are all right?"

"Yes. And I will see you soon."

"I wait! I wait for you!"

I take the phone from Nina.

"Boris," I interrupt, "I've got to talk to Dorothea. We have a lot to discuss, and we don't have much time. Nina's fine. She's with me. I promise to deliver her to you. So now, let me talk to Dorothea. And Rose and you should listen, too."

"Okay, Will, I'm ready," Dorothea says. "What's going on?"

"A whole hell of a lot."

And I tell her what has been happening since Nina and I met at the Moscone Center. I give her all the details, especially the information Nina saw on Kaledin's computer.

"I can't be sure," I say, "but between what Nina remembers she saw on Kaledin's computer…and what I saw on that sketch in his office, I think you and the FBI may have enough probable cause to get a search warrant. Obviously, Kaledin and his Mafia guys are doing *something* with those stores. And it's not end-of-the-month sales."

Then I tell her, "We should be on the road in about a half hour. And back in Los Angeles between seven and eight tonight."

"Will, let's think about this," Dorothea cautions. "If Kaledin is so determined to get to Nina and you, maybe it's not such a good idea for you to bring her directly into Los Angeles tonight."

"Why is that?"

"Because, even with what you've told me, I don't think I can get things going – until at least tomorrow. I mean, our office has been playing very tight on this Russian Mafia investigation. Lots of manpower. High level interest. You know the drill. What Nina and you have is interesting. But it's not hard proof of anything. If you had actual files taken from his computer, that'd be different. But you don't. So this all may take a little longer."

What Dorothea is saying makes sense. And I suspect I'll get the same reaction from Charlie Black, whom I'm going to call right after I finish talking to Dorothea. Even trading heavily on our friendship, I can't ask Charlie to go out on too long a limb and ask his captain for special protection for Nina and Boris, just like that. Nina and I would have to convince Charlie and his superiors, before we could hope to get LAPD to take any action.

"I've got an idea," Dorothea interrupts my thinking.

"All ideas gratefully accepted."

Dorothea tells me, "I have a cabin up at Big Bear. You could take Nina and stay there, until I can arrange something with the Bureau."

I think about it. Then, "Sounds right to me. Listen. I know how to get to Big Bear. But then, how do we get to your place?"

Dorothea gives me directions, which I write down in the small note pad I always carry with me. A habit from my LAPD days, to keep the details of whatever case I was handling at the time.

"And how do we get in?"

"There are several flowerpots on the front porch. The second pot to the right of the front door has a key under it. Also, the electricity is on, but the phone is disconnected."

"My portable phone won't work up there?" I ask.

"No, it won't."

"Any store or gas station nearby, with a phone?"

"There's a small general store about a half mile before you get to the cabin. You'll see it on your way up. There's a pay phone outside, in a booth. And I know from experience that it does work."

******

Next, I call my ex-partner at LAPD, Charlie Black. I know that Charlie is handling the Paul Andreyov homicide investigation.

"Listen," I tell him when he picks up, "I've got information that ties in with your investigation of the Andreyov homicide. And it's also information that you and Ray Malik are going to love."

I fill Charlie in, with the same information I gave to Dorothea. When I finish, Charlie doesn't reply right away. I'm not worried. I know how Charlie's mind works, when he gets information. Listen. Absorb. Sort. Speak.

And he does speak, when he's ready. And he tells me what I expect to hear.

"Going to take some doing. And some time, to get the lady and her grandfather the kind of protection that counts. Even if the information is good."

"It is," I assure him.

Then I suggest, "Maybe the first thing you should do is talk to Ray Malik and fill him in. This being a Russian Mafia deal, maybe he can get the brass to move faster on this."

"Good point," Charlie agrees.

Then, before hanging up, I give Charlie the details about Dorothea's cabin at Big Bear, where Nina and I will be staying.

Next, it's time to pick up my third rental car – ouch – and head for Los Angeles.

CHAPTER THIRTY-NINE

"Stop walking so much, already. You'll make a hole in the carpet," Rose says to Boris, who is pacing non-stop in his living room.

"I do not worry about holes in the carpet. I worry only about my Nina."

Rose pats the couch where she is sitting.

"Come. Sit down," she urges Boris.

When he does, Rose takes his hand in both of hers.

"You heard Nina on the phone. She's safe. She is with Will. And he knows what to do," Rose assures Boris.

He sighs.

"I am an old man, Rose. I got no future, except when I see my Nina. Then, I look forward to tomorrow."

He shakes his head.

"But when I don't see Nina, I don't see no tomorrow."

"Then you and I have the same objective," the voice from the living room entrance startles Rose and Boris.

"To see Nina, as soon as possible," Aleksi Kaledin continues, pointing his gun at them, the silencer attached.

"You!" Boris growls, starting to get up from the couch.

"Boris! No!" Rose shouts, trying to keep him on the couch.

Kaledin points his weapon directly at Boris.

"Listen to her, Boris. Or I'll shoot you right now!"

Reluctantly, Boris sits back down.

"What do you want?" he grumbles at Kaledin.

Kaledin smiles.

"The same thing you want, Boris. To see Nina. So, I think it would be a good idea for you to tell me where she is."

CHAPTER FORTY

Dorothea glances anxiously at her watch. She's been gone from Boris's house a bit longer than she'd intended. Had to pick up some things at the market. Boris kept a bare refrigerator. So there was nothing in the house to eat for dinner. And everyone was hungry.

She turns left on to Boris's street and drives toward his house, halfway down the block and on the left. She was going to park in his driveway but then she spots the car parked in front of the house. It's a late model, black, four-door Mercedes, and she notices it because the vehicle differs so much from the surrounding Toyotas, Hondas, Fords, and trucks that are more typical of this neighborhood.

The presence of the Mercedes doesn't feel right to Dorothea. And there also is something about the car that bothers her.

Then she realizes what it is. It's Aleksi Kaledin's car! She saw it enough times when she had him under surveillance at Futura Furniture.

Dorothea drives her car into a parking place on the side of the street opposite Boris's house. She gets out of the car. Drawing her weapon from her shoulder holster, she crosses the street and approaches Boris's house from the next door neighbor's driveway.

When she reaches the edge of Boris's house, she works her way along the front, until she is at the living room windows.

She looks in and she sees Aleksi Kaledin standing in front of the couch, pointing his weapon at Rose and Boris.

Inside, an increasingly agitated Kaledin says to Boris, "I don't believe you! I'm sure you know where Nina is. I know it! And you will tell me! Or I will kill you!"

"He doesn't know!" A concerned Rose shouts – worried about what Kaledin is going to do.

"You be quiet! Or you'll be dead, too!" Aleksi threatens.

Aleksi glares at Boris.

"I'm waiting for your answer."

He raises his weapon so that it is level with Boris's forehead and just a few inches away from it.

"Put the gun down! Now!" Dorothea orders Kaledin. She has managed to get into the house without Kaledin hearing her, and she is standing in the archway to the living room.

"FBI," she identifies herself. "Federal Bureau of Investigation. I have my weapon pointed at you, and I command you to put down your gun and raise your hands."

Perhaps Kaledin doesn't believe Dorothea. Or maybe he does believe her, but he wants to see her. Whatever the reason, while still pointing his weapon at Boris, Kaledin half turns, toward Dorothea.

To her dismay, Dorothea sees Boris start to get up from the couch, the anger clear on his face, as he lunges at the now half-turned Kaledin.

Dorothea wants to fire at Kaledin, but Rose and Boris are physically so close to him, that she's concerned about injuring them.

She can only watch, as Boris begins to swing at Kaledin.

Kaledin senses Boris's attack, and he turns back, just in time to bring his gun butt down on Boris's head, sending him to the ground.

Rose screams as Boris falls.

Kaledin spins back toward Dorothea and fires two rounds.

They miss, as Dorothea falls away from the doorway but still hesitates to fire. Still concerned that Rose and Boris are in the line of fire.

Kaledin rushes Dorothea and again swings his gun butt, this time on Dorothea's head. She manages to avoid most of the blow, but enough of the butt makes contact, knocking her to the ground, as Kaledin runs out of the house.

CHAPTER FORTY-ONE

Gregor Ramikin listens to the telephone caller.

"Yes," he says, "Aleksi was here earlier. I gave him the information."

He listens again – and now, a look of disbelief comes to his face.

"That idiot!"

He listens again.

"Yes, I agree. Yes. Right away!"

CHAPTER FORTY-TWO

Charlie Black is at his desk. He's been off duty since four in the afternoon, and it is now well into the evening. But he's stayed at his desk, worried about his ex-partner and good friend, Will.

He considers what he should do. It's tricky. No doubt about it. But he has a hunch.

He smiles at his thoughts. He has a hunch, huh?

That's what Will had always called those moments when one or the other of them would think of some fact, some angle, that would bring them out of the fog on an investigation, and point them in the right direction toward solving the case.

Well, I'm operating strictly on hunches now, Charlie admits to himself. And if I'm wrong, then a good part of my ass will be cut off by the Department.

But if I'm right – then I can't ignore what I'm thinking.

So I don't really have any choice, do I?

Chapter Forty-Four

Big Bear, along with nearby Lake Arrowhead, are two of the reasons Southern Californians are envied, or hated, take your choice, by those less fortunate folks in other parts of the country, who have to slog through those miserable winters.

While they're putting on ten layers of clothes, and those rubber galoshes that refuse to slide over their shoes, we have it better, much better out here in God's country.

Want milder temperatures in January? Stay right here in the City of the Angels. Or scoot on down to an even warmer place, like Palm Springs or another of the desert communities.

But suppose you want snow. Want to ski. No problem. Strap those skis to the top of your car and head up to Big Bear, only a couple of hours away. Plenty of snow up there.

Of course, the real nuts in the City of Angels are those who surf Malibu in the A.M., and then are skiing Big Bear that afternoon. It's true. It can be done. Check it out.

But back to reality. And right now, that means Nina and I getting out of San Francisco without any of Kaledin's Korps following us. Usually, that would mean taking Highways 5 or 101 – the fastest routes back. But I want to avoid the usual – that's how they'd expect us to go. And instead, I take Highway 1, and I keep checking the rear-view mirror for tails – but don't spot any.

The 1 takes us to I-14, then to I-15 – and finally, corkscrew winding Highway 18 up into the San Bernardino Mountains, past Lake Arrowhead, to Big Bear.

In addition to the skiing in the surrounding mountain slopes, Big Bear also has a lake called, guess what, Big Bear Lake.

But Nina and I aren't going to one of the many houses dotted around that body of water.

Instead, following Dorothea's directions, we take a narrow road out of Big Bear City and eventually reach the cabin. Isolated. Off by itself.

"No neighbors," Dorothea had told me.

And that suited Nina and me just fine. Like that movie star once said, we "Vant to be alone." At least until Dorothea and Charlie do their things with the Bureau and the LAPD, and can safely bring us in to Los Angeles.

On the drive from San Francisco, I'd given Nina a pad and pencil I always carried with me. It was a habit from my days with the LAPD, when I was working a case and wanted to keep notes.

I told her, "Write down everything you remember from what you saw on Kaledin's computer. We're going to need that information in our discussions with the FBI and the Los Angeles Police Department. I'll do the same, once we get to where we're going."

Now, at Big Bear, I tell Nina, "Give me the pad, with the notes you've written down from the computer."

"Why?" she asks.

I can't blame her for being concerned and not exactly anxious to give me what she's written. She's been through a lot. And I'm sure she feels those notes of hers are all that stand between her and Kaledin.

I explain, "Because I want to hide the notes out there," I say, nodding toward the woods that surround the clearing around the cabin.

My answer frightens Nina.

"This means you expect Aleksi to find us here?"

"No. I don't expect Kaledin to show up. But we need to plan for that possibility.

"So, let's just suppose he does come here. And he finds the pad on you, with your notes. He'll know that you don't have any file that you took off of his computer."

"How will he know this?"

"What I saw about Kaledin, when we met – is that he's a logical guy. So I would expect his reasoning to go like this.

"If you *do* have any notes on you, then this means you *don't* have any file that you took off of his computer.

"But if you *don't* have any notes on you, then this means you *do* have a computer file – just like you originally told him you did – and you've hidden it.

"See the difference?"

Nina considers my explanation. She doesn't like it. But she realizes it makes sense.

She puts her hand in her coat pocket, takes out the pad and pencil, and gives them to me. I look around the car and spot the plastic takeout bag from the food stop we made along the way. I wrap the pad in it. Don't want it to get wet, when I bury it in the woods.

"You stay here," I tell her. "I don't want you to know where I'm hiding this."

My idea is to get Nina off the hook if Kaledin somehow does find us. If she doesn't know where the pad is, and I do, then the heat will be on me, not her. Not that I'm any kind of hero. Believe me, I don't look forward to Kaledin's questioning tactics, but hey, this is why I get paid the big bucks.

"No," Nina says, "I must know where the pad with the notes is."

I can see Nina is not going to give in on this point.

So, "Come on," I tell her, as I start walking toward the woods at the rear of the cabin.

We wander through the dense brush until I find what I want – a bush that I'll be able to recognize later. The last thing I need is to hide the pad, and then not be able to find it.

There are several layers of leaves around the bush, and I clear them away, until I reach the bare earth. I take the pad in its plastic bag and shove it into the tangle of branches that form the base of the bush, managing to get the bag far enough in so that it can't be seen.

I pile the leaves back around the bush and step away, to check things out. Good. Everything looks the way it should.

CHAPTER FORTY-THREE

Now, Nina and I go back to the front of the cabin. Dorothea had told me the key was under the second flowerpot to the right of the front door. And there it is.

I open the door, we go in, and after I find the light switch on the wall, I look around.

Typical Big Bear setup. Plain and comfortable.

We are in the main, high-ceilinged, all-purpose room. A couch and easy chairs are off to the side, facing a large fireplace, with a couple of area rugs covering the wood floor.

A small kitchen is along the other wall, with a square, four-seat table. At the rear of the main room there is a hallway, off of which there are two bedrooms and a bathroom.

Large picture windows on both sides of the front door, and smaller windows flanking the fireplace. Another window over the kitchen sink.

Back on the I-14, I'd picked up sandwiches and sodas, and Nina and I now sit down to eat our feast.

As we eat, I take a good look at her. She looks beat to hell, and I figure she can't take much more of the strain she is under.

"It'll all be over soon," I tell her, hoping to give her a bit of a lift. "By tomorrow, it will all be over."

"I wish I could believe it will be so," she says wistfully. She smiles. "And you will be able to protect Boris and me? Just like that?"

I nod. "Just like that," I assure her.

Okay – what did you want me to say? Tell her it was going to be a ball buster to pull all that off? I knew that. But it was possible. So I wasn't about to paint a black, or even a gray, picture for Nina right now. Not the way she was feeling.

After we eat, we check out the bedrooms. Nina takes one, me the other.

A short while after she goes to her room, I check on Nina. She's asleep. The girl is exhausted.

CHAPTER FORTY-FOUR

It's now close to ten o'clock and I think about going back down toward Big Bear City, to that telephone booth outside the general store. When we first came to it, I tried to call Dorothea on Boris's telephone, at his home, where Rose, Dorothea, and Boris were staying. No answer, which worries me. Where could they be?

I think I'd better go back to that telephone booth and try again.

But no, I tell myself. I really can't do that. Can't leave Nina alone. I just can't.

Instead, I lie down on my bed, figuring I'm not going to sleep. Just rest a little.

I guess I did doze off for a while, but then I'm awakened by some lights that keep going on and off, on and off.

What the hell?

I sit up and look at the luminescent dial of my watch. It's 11:30.

Nina runs into my room, scared.

"What is that light going on and off?" she cries. "What is happening?"

"I'm going to find out right now," I tell her. "You stay here."

I take my gun out of the holster that I'd draped over the bed post, leave the bedroom and work my way down the hallway. The damn light from outside keeps going on, off, on, off.

By the time I reach the central room of the cabin, I know what the light source is. There's a car out there, its headlights flicking on and off.

Someone wants us to know they are outside the cabin.

Kaledin! Somehow, his people managed to tail us out of San Francisco. I can't figure how. I could swear on that stack of bibles. Old or New Testament, or both, that no one had followed us!

Wait a minute! If it's Kaledin, he wouldn't announce himself by flicking his car lights. That doesn't make any sense.

So, who the hell is out there?

I go across the room to one of the windows at the side of the front door and peek out.

And what do I see?

Boris!

Standing in front of a car, in front of the headlights. Boris. Waving.

I open the front door and go out on to the porch.

"What the hell are you doing here?" I ask the obvious question.

Boris gestures toward the car behind him.

"You got to ask Miss FBI Lady."

CHAPTER FORTY-FIVE

A short while later, we're sitting in the cabin – Nina, Boris, Rose, Dorothea, and me – as Dorothea tells us about Kaledin coming to Boris's house and what happened.

"So I thought this would be the safest place right now. Out of Los Angeles. Away from Kaledin until tomorrow, when I can get everyone on board at the Bureau. And coordinate with the LAPD, with your friend, Detective Black."

"You sure you weren't followed?" I ask.

Dorothea considers my question.

"I didn't see any tail. I don't think we were followed."

By now, it is well after midnight, but it doesn't look like any of us are going to do much sleeping.

Nina, Boris, and Rose are on the couch, Boris and Nina holding hands and smiling at each other. While Rose looks on – but mainly at Boris. Yes, there *is* something developing there.

Dorothea and I go back to my bedroom, to plan our actions for tomorrow.

"I figure I'll go down to that telephone at the general store about 11:00 tomorrow morning," I say. "By then, Charlie should have something – hopefully something good – to tell me, about LAPD's involvement."

"There should be some word, too, about the Bureau's involvement," Dorothea says. "I should come with you. So I can check in, there."

I think about it.

"Yeah, I guess it's okay to leave the three of them here. Nothing's going to happen."

My prediction is abruptly upended.

As Nina screams, "No!"

And Boris roars, "You bastard!"

What the hell?

Dorothea and I draw our weapons, bolt out of the bedroom, and run into the main room.

Damn! It's Kaledin. And he's standing next to the couch, his weapon pointed right at Boris's head. Nina and Rose are seated next to Boris, their hands raised.

Kaledin shouts at us. "Drop your guns, or I will kill the old man and the woman."

Dorothea and I don't do as he says. Instead, we train our weapons on Kaledin.

Meanwhile, his gun is about two or three feet from Boris's head.

"Don't be foolish," Kaledin says. He nods at Boris and Rose. "These two will be dead in seconds, if you persist in being foolish. Drop your weapons on the floor and step back. Now!"

Dorothea and I stay still for another few seconds, but then I bend down and put my weapon on the floor.

Dorothea is still holding hers. I look at her, and I see the guilt on her face, as she realizes that Kaledin has managed to follow her to the cabin, despite her certainty that he had not.

I'm concerned that the guilt, along with the anger it is generating, may be clouding Dorothea's thinking. And I suspect she's weighing the chances of firing at Kaledin, even though he has his weapon leveled on Boris.

I talk to her.

"Dorothea, no. You have to put your weapon down."

She looks at me. I nod at the floor. She makes her decision. She bends down and places her gun on the floor.

"Now, sit down on the couch," Kaledin orders.

He smiles.

"Yes, a little crowded. But you're all good friends."

Give the man credit for one thing. He is cool.

"What do you want?" I ask.

"What do you think I want? The file, of course."

Kaledin waves his gun in Boris's direction. "And I'm sure what *you* want is for this old man to stay alive. So…the file? Now!"

Kaledin looks at Nina.

"Come, Nina. Give me the file and then this crazy business will be done."

"Nina doesn't have it. I do," I tell Kaledin.

He looks at me, not sure if he should believe what I'm telling him.

"Oh? And why is it that you have it?"

"Because she gave it to me."

Kaledin is silent for a few seconds. Beside me, I could sense Dorothea surveying the situation, trying to see if there was a way she and I could rush Kaledin, even without our weapons, and overcome him.

I don't think it's possible, but I know that unless I can convince Kaledin that I really do have the file, then Dorothea and I – rushing him together – might be our only chance.

I tell Kaledin, "I'll give you the file if you let everyone go to the back of the cabin. And that's the only way you're going to get it. Believe me, Nina doesn't even know where I have it."

Kaledin isn't quite biting on that...yet.

"How can that be?" he asks suspiciously.

"Because I didn't want something like this to happen. My job is to keep Nina safe. So I took the file away from her. You don't have to hurt her, to get it. I'll give it to you. Just let her go."

Kaledin thinks, then warns me, "No tricks."

"No tricks," I confirm.

"All right," Kaledin says. "You," he says to Dorothea, "get that tape by the door. Slowly and carefully."

I look toward the front door, and just inside it I see a large role of silver duct tape. Kaledin must have brought it with him.

When he sees me look at the tape, Kaledin smiles.

"I am a regular American Boy Scout," he jokes. "Always prepared. And this is *my* plan. No going to the back of the cabin for everyone. Being tied up is better."

Kaledin tells Nina, "Bring the chairs from the kitchen table over to the couch."

When Nina brings the first one over, Kaledin orders Boris to leave the couch and sit in the chair.

"Now," Kaledin tells Nina, "tie him up with the tape. And don't fake it – or I will simply shoot him. Understand?"

Boris moves from the couch to the chair, and with Kaledin giving her instructions on how to tie up Boris, Nina does so.

Kaledin has Nina repeat the process, first for Rose, and then for Dorothea.

"Good. All very good," Kaledin says, as Nina completes her work.

"And now you – into the fourth chair," he orders Nina.

"Jonas," Kaledin tells me, "Tie Nina up. And do it right, or you know the consequences."

After I finish tying up Nina, Kaledin waves his weapon at me.

"And now the file. Give it to me."

"It's not in here. I hid it. Out in the woods."

"I'm tired of your games!" Kaledin shouts.

"I'm not playing games," I say. "I put the file out there, when we first got here. I'm ready to take you to it. Now."

Kaledin looks at me. Decides I'm telling the truth. He motions me toward the door of the cabin.

"Then let us go outside. But carefully. I do not mind shooting you in the back, if necessary."

I don't doubt him for a minute.

I take one last look at Nina, Rose, Dorothea, and Boris, and pray that I can figure out something, once Kaledin and I are out of the cabin. I'm certain that if I cannot, then Kaledin will kill me out there, and then come back inside and finish them off. Hell! He's probably going to do that, anyway!

CHAPTER FORTY-SIX

I walk out of the front door of the cabin, Kaledin right behind me. I pause on the porch, playing for time, as I try to think of a way to get at him.

"Move," Kaledin commands, reinforcing his order by shoving his gun between my shoulder blades.

I go down the steps of the porch and turn left. I go to the corner of the building, turn left and walk along the side of the cabin, to the rear.

Suddenly, there's a rustling sound in the brush, at the edge of the back yard, and involuntarily, I jump back as a large, I don't know what the hell it is, maybe a rat or something, comes scuttling out toward me, before veering off and disappearing back into the brush.

My backwards move propels me into Kaledin's gun.

"Enough with the goddamn poking," I shout. "I don't need reminders."

"What *was* that?" Kaledin says, also obviously as startled as I was by the sudden appearance of the animal.

"I have no idea. Maybe a rat, a raccoon, I don't know."

Hey, I'm a city boy. Dogs and cats I can ID, and maybe even an elephant if one wanders into my neighborhood. But my capabilities are pretty much nil beyond that.

I walk toward the brush that borders the back of the house, Kaledin right behind me. And as I take each step, I wonder if I should suddenly stop, twist around, and go at Kaledin.

Would I surprise him enough so that he wouldn't get any shots off? Or if he did, would he have time to aim?

We reach the edge of the brush and I stop.

"It's in there," I tell Kaledin, indicating the brush.

"So, go," he says.

I walk into the brush, Kaledin right behind me.

And an idea starts to form in my mind.

Although I recognize the correct bush right away, I don't go for it. Instead, I keep walking around, playing for more time. I want to get Kaledin upset. When someone is upset, they get sloppy. Maybe not paying as much attention to the details. The more I could put Kaledin into that frame of mind, the better.

"Come on," he says after a few more minutes of my wandering. "You are stalling. Do not try this trick anymore. I want the file. Now!"

I've played out the string as far as I can. I go to the right bush, bend down and clear the leaves away from the base. With my right hand, I reach into the tangle of branches and bring out the note pad wrapped in my handkerchief.

Okay, I decide. Now is when I need to make my move.

I stay in my crouch, shift the pad to my left hand, and extend it to Kaledin.

At the same time, I dig my right hand into the ground around the base of the bush, and get a fistful of moist soil.

Kaledin leans down to take the pad from me.

I whip my right hand up, throw the dirt into his face, and lunge at him.

There's a gunshot.

I expect his bullet to slam into me.

Kaledin stumbles.

His face registers surprise.

The blood starts to gurgle out of his chest.

Kaledin stands motionless for a second. Then he crumples to the ground.

I look beyond Kaledin, into the backyard, wondering if, somehow, Dorothea had gotten free, retrieved her weapon, and followed us out here.

But instead I see two men.

I recognize one of them.

Ray Malik, the Russian Mafia guru at LAPD.

I don't know the other man.

Relief! It's a great feeling.

"Ray! How'd you get here? And am I glad you did!"

Malik smiles, but it's not a friendly smile.

"That may depend," Malik says.

I don't understand. Especially when the other man speaks to me.

"The file. Give it to me."

This guy also isn't smiling.

"Ray, what's going on?" I ask Malik.

"Just business, Jonas. Business you'd have been better off not getting involved in."

I turn to the other guy.

"Hey, I'm one of the good guys." I nod at Kaledin's body. "He's the bad guy, and he's dead."

"As will you be, unless you now hand me that file," the man threatens.

And then it hits me.

This guy has a heavy Russian accent. And he and Malik are definitely a team in this little exercise.

"So that's it, Ray?" I ask Malik. "You've crossed the line?"

"Business is too good on the other side of the line, Will." He nods at the other man. "Meet my partner, Gregor Ramikin."

Uh oh! The alarm goes off in my head.

And I realize that with Malik telling me he's crossed the line, and also giving me Ramikin's name, it can only mean one thing.

They don't care that they've given me this information.

Why?

Simple conclusion.

If I'm dead, I sure can't tell anyone, can I?

And the same holds true for Nina, Boris, Rose, and Dorothea.

They're planning to kill all of us!

I *have* to find a way to stop this from happening!

But my thoughts are cut short by Malik.

"Give the file to Ramikin, Will. Or you're a dead man – right now!"

I give Ramikin the file. And then, urged by Malik and his weapon, I walk around to the front, and into the cabin.

Dorothea, Nina, Rose, and Boris, tied to their chairs, will be easy killing targets.

I have to figure out something!

I try to prolong things by asking questions.

I speak to Malik.

"Why'd you do this, Ray? Why?"

"I already told you," he snaps.

"How'd you know we were here? How'd Kaledin find us?"

Ray shrugs.

"Phone taps are a wonderful thing. We knew every move you were making, from the time you went to San Francisco, up through your last call to the FBI lady, when you discussed coming to this cabin.

"As for Kaledin, he didn't have the phone taps, and so his guys lost you at the hotel in San Francisco."

"Then it wasn't Kaledin's people who came at us in the Moscone Center?" I ask.

"No, it was Ramikin's crew," Malik says.

"But the first guy I spotted in the Center was someone I saw when I met with Kaledin at Futura."

Ramikin laughs.

"Aleksi thought that was one of his. But the man really works for me. Keeps me up to date on what Aleksi is always doing."

"So, how did Kaledin know we were here?"

Malik says, "We made the mistake of telling him about the cabin. Never thought he'd be stupid enough to come up here on his own."

"Ray," Ramikin says, "enough talking. We have things to do."

He reaches into his jacket and brings out a weapon.

Then they nod at each other and raise their weapons.

Ray aims at me.

Ramikin aims at Dorothea.

The front door slams open!

"Weapons down now!" someone shouts.

And Charlie Black and four uniforms burst into the cabin, everyone carrying a police version of an AK 47 automatic weapon.

For a couple of seconds, it's a standoff.

Then Malik and Ramikin realize it's hopeless.

They put their weapons on the floor and raise their hands.

CHAPTER FORTY-SEVEN

"How did you know we were here? And that Malik had turned bad?" I pepper Charlie with my questions.

The San Bernardino Sheriff's Department deputies – those were the four uniforms with Charlie – had taken Malik and Ramikin to their lockup facility for the night. We were all still in the cabin.

Charlie grins.

"Hunches, Will. Hunches," he says.

Dorothea says, "Look…I know you two were partners for a long time. And so you can talk in shorthand like that. But how about letting the rest of us in on it?"

"When we were partners," I explain, "Charlie and I would be working a case, getting nowhere, and then one of us would have a hunch. And that usually opened things up."

I ask Charlie, "I guess you had some good hunches here, huh? Like, how did you know Malik was dirty?"

"I started putting things together after you told me about your experience with Kaledin," Charlie answers, "and after Andreyov was killed. And then his widow.

"With all this going on, it seemed to me that it made no sense for Ray Malik, as our Russian Mafia guru, not to know more than he seemed to know. That's when I started getting suspicious about him."

I think back to my own last conversation with Malik, when I'd tried to fill him in on my meeting with Kaledin. All he kept saying at the time was, "Interesting." I had chalked that up to the fact that he was in the middle of an investigation and didn't want to share anything confidential with me, since I was no longer LAPD.

I tell Charlie and the others that now, and Charlie nods.

"That figures. You showing up, looking for Nina, that really was screwing things up for Malik and Ramikin, not to mention Kaledin."

"But how did you know about tonight?" Dorothea asks. "I mean, how did you know to come here? To follow Malik here?"

"That was my wildest hunch of all. And a major gamble, at that, because it put all of you in danger."

"What do you mean?" I ask.

"Well, after you called me, Will, and told me where you and Nina were going to be tonight, I called Malik. I told him everything you had told me. About the file. About Kaledin. About your bringing Nina in. Everything. The only thing I didn't tell him, was that Nina did not have any actual file from Kaledin's computer. I knew that was too important to let him know about.

"Anyway, I figured, if he's straight, then he'd act accordingly. Take up a whole team of detectives, contact the San Bernardino

Sheriff's Department, and coordinate a fast trip up here, to meet you and to start to give you and Nina the protection you needed."

"But he didn't do that," I say.

"No, he didn't," Charlie answers. "And as soon as I saw that, I knew I had to get up here. I pulled some favors with the San Bernardino Sheriff's Department, to get the backup firepower I needed, and up we came.

"Oh. And one more thing, Will. Before I left, I set up 24-hour, on-site protection for Lu. Two guys are there right now. Outside your condo. And I'm not going to pull them off until we all get back to Los Angeles."

Nina asks, "It is good now? My grandfather? Me? We can be protected now?"

Charlie nods.

"Speaking for the LAPD, my answer is yes."

I look at Dorothea.

"And what about the FBI?" I ask her.

She nods.

"I've got to put all this through the system. But considering how much we've wanted to nail these people, and what you and Will can give us, I'm sure everything will work out just fine for your grandfather and you."

Boris comes into the conversation now, addressing me.

"I know I pick the right master detective when I pick you," he says.

"Master detective, Will?" Charlie repeats Boris's words. "I know you were an LAPD Homicide detective. And then you became a private detective. But a master detective? That's a new one. Is there some sort of a license for that, Will?"

I look at Charlie.

"Show respect," I tell him.

"Why should I start now?" he answers back.

"Because he is older than you," Rose comes to my defense.

Um...

"Rose," I say, "I know you mean well, but...

ABOUT THE AUTHOR

After careers as a broadcast journalist and then a public relations counselor, Saul Warshaw, is now happily enjoying his third career as a writer. Saul has had several of his novels published. Each features Will Jonas, a private investigator and former homicide detective with the Los Angeles Police Department. He's also had two additional novels published, Instinct for Survival and The Eviction Party. Saul and his wife, both native New Yorkers, are longtime residents of Los Angeles. If you would like to write Saul, please do so at: swarshaw0@gmail.com

www.ingramcontent.com/pod-product-compliance
Lightning Source LLC
Chambersburg PA
CBHW072355020726
47506CB00004B/1126